LUCKY STARS

THE ALICE LUCK SPACE ADVENTURES
BOOK 1

H. CLAIRE TAYLOR

FFS
≡ MEDIA ≡

ISBN: 978-1-959041-02-3 (H. Claire Taylor)

FFS Media, LLC

www.ffs.media

contact@hclairetaylor.com

CONTENTS

PROLOGUE

Out there in the universe's deep recesses—in one that was truly no deeper nor shallower than any particular recess—a secretive cloister of synaptically active beings gathered. Their kind, they knew, had held this same gathering since T = 5678!, though what unit of measurement belonged to that quantity of time was unknown, and the digits didn't resemble anything similar to what you see on this page.

They called themselves the— Well, it's hard to write out in the Roman alphabet, but imagine you were attempting to write the word *hootenanny* in cursive with a feather quill on parchment while riding a mechanical bull. That's about the word we're looking at here.

Roughly translated to English, though, which most things in the multiverse are for reasons you'll soon learn, the group was known as the Lexicographers.

And they were searching for the name of God.

Unlike most Homo sapiens on the inconsequential planet of Blerg VFP69, Lexicographers had a fairly clear idea of what God did and did not account for. What God accounted for was everything, and what it did not account for was everything.

The Lexicographers did not, however, bother calling it God. They thought it would be silly to name something before they had discovered its name, and so they generally referred to it as "that force everywhere and nowhere" or "the reason my wife left me."

Usually, though, the reason Lexicographers' wives left them was that they were sick of hearing about God. It was tedious stuff, that everywhere-nowhere nonsense, and wives were a precious commodity.

(I use the term "wife" loosely. Throughout most of the multiverse, it refers more to a being who thanklessly cleans up another being's messes, carries more than their fair share of emotional burdens, and occasionally predicts supernovas in nearby galaxies. See? Nothing like what we on Blerg VFP69 understand a wife to be.)

On this particular starlit planetary rotation, hidden away in the darkness of a cave, two of the Lexicographers prepared to share the first major breakthrough since $T = 5678!$ with their fellow lonely scientists whose wives had recently left them.

Over the course of untold stellar orbits, via painstaking calculations of the building blocks of energy, and through uncountable messy divorces, the pair of Lexicographers had completed their first calculation for the name of God.

Not only that, these two had checked their work.

They stood at the center of the fire-lit cavern as their associates gathered 'round, filling the circular stone seating of the symposium. Off the cave walls echoed a murmur that was mostly composed of a clearing of throats and muffled burping, since, for whatever reason, most sentient beings in existence have evolved loose esophagi and over-acidic stomachs.

Their group included beings from all over, parsecs and light-years away. Such biodiversity had, in the early days, cost the tailor in charge of fashioning the coarse black robes for each member much lost sleep. But by now the variation was an accepted stressor of the job, and the tailor was much less of a perfectionist; as long as it was loose enough and had the right number of limb and tentacle holes, he called it done.

On the whole, the Lexicographers preferred not to use advanced technology, opting instead to write out the equations in longhand on bumpy cave walls. Perhaps that had played a part in why it took so long to find the first letter of God's name, but the universal truth held, regardless of inconvenience, that intellectuals and technology were locked in a battle to the death where the winner was ego and everyone else was a loser.

The pair of Lexicographers with the big announcement weren't feeling especially short on ego themselves, after what they'd confirmed, and so they thought a little razzle-dazzle was in order. They brought in a light projector.

And upon those same bumpy walls where they had stubbornly written equation after equation, proof after proof, they projected their recent findings.

The onlooking Lexicographers gasped and belched and broke into reflux-related coughing attacks when they saw what was there.

It wasn't the name of God projected upon the walls, but it was a start.

The two Lexicographers, who fully expected their names to go down in history but have already been forgotten—let's call them Dale and Hammy—revealed what they believed to be the first letter in the name of God.

Unfortunately, neither Dale nor Hammy had any idea what alphabet they were dealing with. Minor detail.

"Ta-da!" they said to kick off the oral presentation.

That was the only remark they'd prepared, though.

While the others stared and grunted, the two Lexicographers of the hour, whatever their names were, grinned proudly.

"But what does it mean?" shouted a cloaked being who resembled a human's sphincter.

"It is the answer! It is the first letter of the name!" replied Dale.

"In what alphabet?" shouted the sphincter.

"We have no idea." Dale grinned.

As the chorus of bodily noises died down, someone in the back stood up on four of his seven legs, which protruded long past the bottom hem of his cloak (it had been "one of those days" for the tailor when he fashioned that particular garment), and declared, "I'll be damned! I believe that might be part of the Roman alphabet. I even suspect the name of God might turn out to be in English!"

No one was happy about that possibility, but in the end, they decided that it sort of figured, what with the ways things had gone in the multiverse so far.

The Lexicographers were among the few groups who had successfully resisted learning the official tongue of the Depot, and while that was usually a point of elitist pride, it left them in a bit of a pickle.

Why in God's name would God's name be in *English*?

They would need to do the math to figure it out.

And that meant they would be late for dinner.

So, those who still had wives sent word back not to wait

up for them (this was a win-win for everyone involved), while those who no longer had wives harshly judged those who still did for not being truly committed to the Lexicographer mission.

Amid it all, a single symbol remained projected onto the cave wall. The first letter of God's true name.

It looked like this:

H

CHAPTER
ONE

The planet of Blerg VFP69 is so minuscule a part of its universe as to be mathematically negligible. But so is any first cancer cell.

The life there remained self-contained for millions of years, and then one day, it started shooting bits of itself into space. Little chunks of organic debris, first with tails and then without, and each of them either returned to the planet or burned to bits. Either was good news for all non-Blerg VFP69 life.

And then, someone did something very stupid.

That person was a life-form from Blerg MP43 named Droopid, which is a coincidence.

Due to a series of brain traumas, Droopid had developed a fascination with the life on Blerg VFP69 and found their attempts to make it to space simply adorable. He wanted to help them. So, against his better judgment—which was poor to begin with—he did. And suddenly a few dozen of those life-forms without tails left the planet, quite in secret, and most of them did not return *or* burn up.

Droopid realized what he'd done too late. And when the

elders on Blerg MP43 found out, they dissolved him into tiny bits because they wanted to, not because it could fix anything.

Though Blerg VFP69 has made its way around its embarrassingly small sun many times since Droopid's visit, most everything and everyone on the planet has carried on, ignorant of the universe-changing event.

For instance:

Walking over scalding, star-heated asphalt, hardly more than a little dot on the surface of Blerg VFP69, Alice Luck crossed the mostly empty parking lot toward her eleventh job interview of the week.

In a lot of ways, this one was like all the rest. Part of her hoped she would be rejected again and could continue living her post-college life jobless and free to do as she pleased until her third credit card set a firm boundary. When that time came, she would simply start on the fourth credit card. It wasn't her fault folks kept giving her credit cards when she *clearly* couldn't be trusted with them.

Besides, what was a little more debt when she was eighty thousand in the hole on student loans? An excuse to cross the border to Mexico and start fresh? Don't threaten her with a good time. Dying her golden blonde hair brown would be a small price to pay for an exciting life on the lam.

In other crucial ways, however, this job interview was *nothing* like the previous ten had been. For one, it had specifically listed "bachelor's degree or higher in animal husbandry" as a qualification. None of the others had.

The first ten only indicated that holding a four-year degree would be "a plus." Alice had a four-year degree in theory, even if it'd taken her eight years to complete it.

And so, she'd applied to all those jobs, thinking she would make the cut, only to watch the expressions of her interviewers change once their eyes traveled down her CV and they realized that her impressive Bachelor of Science wasn't in chemistry or physics or even psychology, but rather was a degree entirely devoted to getting farm animals knocked up.

This job posting, though, had specifically requested an education in animal husbandry.

So, she couldn't understand why the interview would take place in a giant office supply store like the one she was approaching as she crossed the scorching parking lot.

The mystery was weird enough to keep her interest and shady enough to be worth the effort of dressing like a professional.

She entered through the automatic doors and inhaled the delicious scent of paper, ink, and sanitizer. A snaggletoothed older gentleman greeted her as she looked around for where she was supposed to be.

"Howdy, ma'am. What can I help you find?"

"I'm here for a job interview."

"Ah, I'm afraid we ain't hiring at the moment. But if you want to fill out an app—"

"She's here for me," came a smooth but curt voice, and Alice spotted a woman hurrying down the main aisle toward her, passing large cardboard displays of back-to-school items.

"Liz Windsor," the woman said, offering her hand long before she was within arm's reach of Alice. Finally, she made it close enough, and the two women shook.

Liz Windsor's raven hair was pulled back in a tight roll, emphasizing cheekbones that could cut glass, and piercing sea-blue eyes to match. Alice thought she'd caught hints of a British accent in the woman's first few words, and as Liz Windsor addressed the snaggletoothed greeter, Alice's suspicions were confirmed. "I've got it from here, Liam. Thank you." The snaggletoothed man shuffled off. "You must be Miss Luck."

Alice nodded.

"Great, follow me." Liz Windsor quickstepped back the way she'd come, and Alice was left scrambling to catch up. But just as soon as she'd started, Liz Windsor came to a sudden halt by one of the displays. "Please help yourself to one of the permanent markers. Any color you like."

"Really?" In middle school, after she'd drawn one too many sets of inaccurately proportioned male genitalia on desks, Alice's teachers had been put on notice that they were to take away any permanent marker she might get her hands on. Once her father caught wind of the new rule and what precipitated it, the whoopin' she received had knocked any future thoughts of permanent markers right from her head.

A *whoopin'* is a thing that happens to the smallest and most vulnerable of Blerg VFP69's Homo sapiens inhabitants when they break a rule. The larger, more sexually mature of the species inflict pain upon the little ones out of love and a respect for the rules. It is a time-honored tradition of their kind. Alice Luck had received many of them over the course of her twenty-six years on the planet, because following the rules and having fun rarely overlapped. That was, of course, by design.

Liz Windsor blinked. "Yes, truly. *Any* color."

Alice stepped closer to it and had extended her hand toward a clump of maroon pens when the other woman added, "Choose wisely."

"On what criteria?"

Liz Windsor offered a toothy grin, her high-intensity

eyes forgetting to play along. "The one most important to you."

Alice, not generally one to overthink, rolled her shoulders back then plucked a double-sided fuchsia one from the display. The label had it marked as "radical redshift." Good enough.

She uncapped the thick end and gave it a good sniff on the off chance that it was one of the scented kind. It smelled like dirty feet and milk breath, and she was forced to concede that she didn't know what radical redshift smelled like and therefore wasn't able to determine if this was a scented marker or not.

"*Very* interesting choice, Miss Luck," said Liz Windsor, and Alice turned to find that the woman appeared … impressed. "You're the first one to *sniff* the marker." Still impressed. No hint of sarcasm. "I don't want to get ahead of myself, but I have a good feeling about you already. Follow me."

The strange woman entered a hallway at the back of the cavernous store that said it led to the restrooms, and Alice found she wouldn't be surprised if that was where the interview took place. Nothing about this job opportunity made any goddamn sense to her. Not the degree requirement, not the location, and certainly not the permanent marker selection. She suspected nothing could surprise her at this point.

She was wrong.

Liz Windsor led them past the bathroom entrances and through a door marked Employees Only. But she didn't stop there. Past the towering boxes of inventory stood another door, this one with a sign beside it reading Not Even Employees Past This Point.

Who *was* allowed?

Liz Windsor, it seemed, and now Alice as well.

Beyond the door, a set of stairs led down—and this was perhaps the strangest thing Alice had encountered yet, because any local knew you hit bedrock six inches down in this part of Texas. No one in their right mind would shell out to drill through all the caliche unless they were desperate to build a shelter from radioactivity or zombies, or both.

Which told her that these people, whose job posting she'd found on an internet site known more for organizing anonymous back-alley hookups than launching anyone's legitimate career, were not in their right mind.

She would be furious if it turned out Jacob was right about this and she ended up murdered.

Down the stairs she went anyway, and soon they stepped into another long, fluorescently lit hallway. Liz Windsor paused, opened a door on their left, and invited Alice inside.

It was a warm space, decorated more like an opium den than the manager's office of an office supply store, but she had a sneaking suspicion she wasn't in Paper Depot anymore.

On the other side of a round wooden table sat a man with the most rigid posture Alice had seen since Jacob invited his boss and boss's wife over for dinner and did his best to show them why he was Junior Vice President of Customer Relations material. But during that whole miserable evening, she'd seen a gleam of panic in her straight-backed boyfriend's eyes, a gleam that was absent from this man's expression.

In fact, almost everything was absent from this man's expression, even though he wore a large, friendly smile. "You must be Alice Luck."

He wasn't unattractive, and looked to be only a few years

her senior, but was, on the whole, disconcertingly put together. There was something rubbery about his smooth face and clear complexion. "Yes, I'm Alice. Nice to meet you."

"Ooh," he said, nodding down at the object in her hand. "You're the first one to pick radical redshift."

"And she *sniffed* it, too," Liz Windsor added, closing the door behind her.

The man's eyes enlarged in a mechanical sort of excitement. "You don't say! What did it smell like?"

Alice knew she was emotionally lazy, and that was why she almost always opted for honesty. At least, that was what she'd been told. She went with it this time anyway. "Like feet and milk breath. Or maybe redshift?"

The man threw his head back and laughed, and it reminded her of how a sock puppet might do it, his bottom jaw mostly staying put and the rest of his skull doing all the work. He motioned to a vacant chair across the round table from him, and she took it as Liz Windsor seated herself next to the man.

"I didn't catch your name," Alice said.

"Call me Mike."

"Okay. Nice to meet you, Mike."

Liz Windsor perked up. "Shall we get started?"

Each of the interviewers proceeded to hold a copy of Alice's CV in front of them and inspect it, making little "hmm"s and "ah, I see"s as they went.

Mike peered at Alice over the page. "You're twenty-six?"

"That's right."

He glanced at Liz Windsor. "That seems a little young, don't you think?"

"Yes, but we can fix it."

"How so?"

"With time."

Each then returned to scanning the page, and Alice noticed something odd. Their eyes moved at the same speed, almost like an automatic typewriter tapping on the keys, then *ching* onto the next line. Not only that, but their eyes also moved in sync with one another's.

They reached the bottom of her CV, where she'd tried to bury the bad stuff.

"Your GPA," Liz Windsor said, and Alice's heart sank. "Is that a 2.4 on a scale of zero to 2.4?"

Alice snorted, then when neither of her interviewers showed signs of understanding her reaction, she said, "Yes, that's it."

Mike asked the next question. "And how would you crossbreed a ewe and a tomcat?"

"*Jesus.*" Alice cringed. "I wouldn't."

Mike and Liz Windsor shared an overly appreciative nod. "She seems to know her stuff," Mike added.

Liz Windsor smiled at Alice. "Do you have any questions for us?"

"Yes. The job responsibilities on the posting were—well, some of them were puzzling."

"Go on."

Alice slipped her phone from the pocket of her slacks and pulled up the listing. "Cultural sensitivity, I get. And a more culturally sensitive person, you will not find. But this one ... I don't know what specifically it's referring to. It says, 'Good aim.' Is that with ... ideas? Or, like, a firearm or ...?"

Mike's cheery expression didn't change as he said, "It's with everything. We need someone who has good aim in every sense of the word."

"Ah." Feeling more confident, she leaned back in her

chair. The Jacob that lived in her head sighed heavily at her poor posture. "Well, I do know my way around a rifle, being a Texas girl and all."

Liz Windsor's face morphed, and for a split second, Alice thought she'd said something wrong. But quite the contrary. "Hold on. You are *originally* from Texas? Born and raised here? A *genuine* Texan?"

"Yep."

Mike licked his lips, but hardly seemed able to contain the excitement behind his shiny exterior.

"One more question," Alice said, careful not to take her eyes off the strange man. "It also says the job requires frequent travel. How frequent are we talking?"

"Almost entirely," said Liz Windsor. "Lots of commuting. But you won't be alone. You'll be traveling with your team. Would that be a problem for you?"

"Not at all. I love travel." Alice thought about starting over in Mexico. She'd always liked the name Gabriella. Gabriella Rosado? Not a bad alias if it came to that. But maybe it wouldn't. If she got this job, maybe disappearing wouldn't be the only way to knock out her student loans.

"Student loans" are a rite of passage for juvenile Homo sapiens in the geographical location known as the United States. Under the dire threat of whoopin's, Homo sapiens who have reached the arbitrary age of maturity and undergone an extensive intellectual grooming process are pressured into continuing the academic process. Under extreme duress, natural predators gift the youngling a currency that they pay to the academic institution and then must also repay to their natural predators, usually threefold. It is a time-honored tradition of their kind. Alice owed $79,854 at the time of her interview. If she started over in Mexico, she would owe $0.

Mike's brows pinched together, and Alice had never seen such a straight crease on a forehead before. "One more question for you, Miss Luck."

She waited for it as his eyes scanned over a few lines in the middle of her CV.

"How might you crossbreed a ram and a dung beetle?" He stared at her unblinkingly.

"I would *never* try that."

"My God, she's good!" Liz Windsor proclaimed.

Mike's expression broke into a sly grin and he slowly clapped.

"Magnificent," he added. "Amazing. You see how she didn't even have to think about it? I think she might be a natural."

"Now, now. Let's not get ahead of ourselves," Liz Windsor warned.

"I hate to be rude," Alice said, "but is this an hourly position, or salary?"

"Neither. It's project-completion based."

"And what range are we looking at?"

"It's all negotiable," Liz Windsor replied. "When could you start?"

"Any time. I'm not currently working. I could start right now if you wanted."

"Oh, I *do* love your enthusiasm, Miss Luck! Yes, this is all very good to know."

Suddenly and simultaneously the interviewers rose their feet, and Alice scrambled to hers as well.

"It has been a *pleasure*," Mike said. "We still have a few more interviews to conduct, so I can't promise anything, but I do hope we'll see each other again soon." He winked.

Liz Windsor led the way back up the stairs and past the restrooms before leaving Alice with these parting words: "It was a pleasure to meet you, Miss Luck. Regardless of whom we select, we'll be in touch."

In a slight daze but not without some excitement regarding her prospect of employment, Alice strolled down Paper Depot's main aisle. Remembering the permanent marker in her pocket, she paused at the pen display and used her radical redshift to scribble, *Alice was here*.

CHAPTER
TWO

The smell of the large, forgettable two-story home Alice shared with Jacob was far superior to that of the permanent marker she'd absent-mindedly sniffed the whole drive back from her interview. She didn't know why she'd kept on sniffing it as her mind jumped from one abnormality of the interview to another, only that it felt like the right thing to do, and the more she did it, the less she found herself able to focus on the many red flags.

She was lightheaded by the time she crossed the threshold into domesticity. Only, it wasn't her domesticity that filled the air with a savory aroma.

Emptying her pockets, she tossed her keys and wallet into a hand-printed Haitian ceramic bowl by the front door. Jacob had been gifted it as a thank-you for his volunteer efforts down there following one hurricane or another. Or maybe it was an earthquake. Or an outbreak?

With how many times she'd endured his telling the story to guests as they passed the damn thing, she should remember why he'd been down there. But her brain made this fuzzy sound when she sensed he was about to tell a story she'd already heard, and she usually ended up thinking about fast food or Mexico when the brain noise hit.

She stuffed the marker in her back pocket and made for the kitchen.

Jacob didn't notice her at first as he peeled carrots into the sink. He had his earbuds in, no doubt listening to some self-help podcast or another, and wore an apron over the powder-blue button-down he'd worn to work. He couldn't have been home more than half an hour, but he was already deep into making dinner. One might not know it, though, from the complete cleanliness of the countertops. The lunatic cleaned as he cooked.

Jacob set a peeled carrot onto the cutting board by the sink, and, as he gathered up the peelings to toss into the plastic compost bucket he emptied daily, he looked up and found his girlfriend staring at him. "Oh! Alice!" he said too loudly, then yanked out his earbuds to give her his full attention. "I didn't hear you come in."

"What's for dinner?"

"Huh? Oh, this isn't for dinner." He stepped back and allowed her to see the Crock-Pot on the other side of the cutting board. "Prepping a pot roast for lunch tomorrow."

There was little on Blerg VFP69 that Alice hated more than a Crock-Pot meal. While she usually found them to be delicious, any dish that taunted her olfactory glands for eleven hours before she could enjoy it was no friend of hers. "Oh, great. Sounds amazing. Can't wait … for tomorrow."

"Hey, how was the job interview?" He crossed the kitchen and reached for her. She glanced down at his apron, ready to push him back, then realized there wasn't a speck on it.

"Who knows?"

He wrapped his arms around her waist and pulled her close. She caught a whiff of his cologne mingling with the rich scent of roast and fought the urge to drown it out with the foul scent of the permanent marker.

"You know what?" he said, gazing at her, his dark brown eyes doing that thing they'd done time and time again, sucking her in, making her cozy, asking her to think about forever. "You've been working so hard lately, applying to all these different jobs. I can't imagine it's been easy on you. So what if we don't talk about it anymore this evening? You deserve to relax and have someone take care of you. Have *me* take care of you. Which is why I've made us a rooftop reservation at Vive tonight."

She froze. "Tonight?"

He chuckled airily. "Yes, tonight."

"But it's a Tuesday."

"It's Friday," he said gently. "You've been so absorbed and determined to find a job, you lost track of time."

She knew that couldn't be why, because she'd been half-assing the job search at best, hoping that maybe a meteor would take out the earth before someone offered her a boring job she felt inclined to accept. "Vive is the one over on East Seventh, right? Next to the Sloshed and Tanked?" That was her favorite bar by a mile, but she'd never been with Jacob.

"Yes," he said, "right above Chateau d'Aurelius."

"I don't own anything nice enough for that place."

His hold around her waist tightened, and she fought the urge to fight free of it. "Shh, don't you worry." He pouted slightly and slowly wiggled his hips against her stomach. "I'm serious about wanting to take care of you, Al. Go check the bed. I have it all laid out for you." He planted a kiss on her forehead, and she slipped away as soon as his hold loosened.

Upstairs, she found the dress and shoes, and—oh God— even a new expensive bra and underwear laid out for their date. The dress was an emerald silk, and she could practically hear Jacob telling the clerk at whatever boutique he found this thing at, "This color will match her eyes." The shoes, scrappy and nude color, had three-inch heels.

How did Jacob know about nude heels? Was she dating a man with enough awareness and clarity of mind to not only prepare tomorrow's lunch in the Crock-Pot but also to know that nude shoes were currently in fashion?

She might have questioned his sexuality if he hadn't been so intent on pleasing her night after night, going the extra mile to make sure she finished the race before him. He often reminded her of the helpers she'd seen while cheering on her youngest older brother Wyatt at the Special Olympics, the ones who ran a step behind the athletes that needed it, cheering them on the whole way, providing support, and telling them they were doing great and were so impressive.

She felt her throat constrict, and closer inspection of the underwear didn't help. She realized quite quickly that these were period panties. Wait.

Oh my God, I must be about to start.

How did he know and she didn't?

"Not to rush you," he said, appearing in the doorway, "but I got us an early reservation so we have plenty of time to enjoy the beautiful night air together. They have a rotating menu, and tonight they're serving braised pork ribs."

"My favorite," she whispered hopelessly, still staring at the absorbent, bacteria-resistant undergarment.

"I know. And I've heard good things about their jalapeño margaritas."

"Jalapeño margaritas?" she whined helplessly.

"Also your favorite."

"Yuh-huh."

"The dress," he said, "it has a long zipper in the back. Let me know if you need help with it." He ran a hand over his face, upon which she could see no visible stubble, and said, "I'll get a fresh shave in." He winked at her, making it clear that he, once again, had big plans of cheering her over the finish line after dinner.

Alice watched him disappear into their master bath, then looked down at the outfit again. The dress had been smoothed to show no wrinkles, something that was only possible because the bed was kept crisply made whenever Jacob was home.

She thought back to her college apartment. Had she even had a quilt or comforter? All she could remember were those gray sheets. She was pretty sure they hadn't been gray when she'd bought them.

Alice put on the period panties and the uplifting bra and the emerald dress. It all fit perfectly. She didn't need help with the zipper. She could zip herself up like a big girl.

The shoes were exactly her size, too.

As she looked at herself in the full-length mirror, something inside her screamed to get out, and before she knew what she was doing, she'd stepped inside their closet, slipped off the heels, and replaced them with her trusty Texas-flag cowboy boots. The screaming inside her quieted, and she didn't bother looking at herself in the mirror again;

she already knew the red, white, and blue clashed with the emerald. She was glad it did.

When Jacob emerged from the bathroom, face as soft as an infant Homo sapiens' rear end, his gaze dropped to her boots immediately. "Did the heels not fit? I brought in a pair of yours to show the—"

"No, they fit great."

Next came silence, which is often considered threatening to a talkative species such as Homo sapiens that hasn't spent significant time in the natural emptiness of space.

Finally, Jacob said, "Oh, okay," and that ended the conversation about the boots.

A half-hour later, Alice boot-scooted down the sidewalk of East Seventh, Jacob's nurturing and protective arm around her shoulder as she tried not to stare longingly at the party thumping at Sloshed and Tanked.

A small stairway next to the doors for Chateau d'Aurelius led up to the rooftop of Vive, where their table awaited them. They were five minutes late for the reservation, and rather than admonishing her for taking too long to leave the house, Jacob merely winked at the maître d' and said, "Perfection takes time," as he nodded her way.

The maître d' was a thick slab of blonde like Alice herself —square-jawed, strong, built for driving fence posts. Plenty of Texas girls were bred like that, with the blood of Grandma Helga and connected to the land by the generational lie of Native American heritage.

Most men would've confused the two women, Alice was sure, and she wondered briefly if she could pull a quick switcheroo without Jacob noticing. She could enjoy gainful employment in close proximity to Sloshed and Tanked, and the maître d' could have a dream boyfriend who cooked for her, picked out her outfits, owned a beautiful home, and considered performing cunnilingus on his girlfriend as integral a part of his nightly routine as brushing his teeth both before and after said cunnilingus. It seemed like a fair trade.

The maître d' smiled, a highly practiced and joyless thing, like pinning the tail on a donkey with no blindfold on. "It's no problem, sir. Right this way."

Once they were seated at their romantic table for two by the edge of the rooftop and Alice had concluded that it was too high above the street to make a reasonable escape over the side, she took a deep breath, scanned the Austin skyline, and said, "This is nice."

Jacob reached out and took her hands in his. "Yes, it is. Alice, you look beautiful. You always look beautiful, but tonight … You take my breath away. I know you still see yourself as a country girl, but you're so much more than that."

She forced herself to meet his gaze, and when she did, she felt herself soften and only then realized how prickly she'd been about him all day.

This was Jacob. He loved her, and she most likely loved him back. He never asked for anything from her, only gave. She'd never met anyone quite like that. He knew her needs better than even she did. Hell, she was pretty sure she'd started her period in the car ride over, and were it not for his eerie foresight, her emerald dress would've had a wine-colored spot on the back at that very moment.

It was creepy, yes, but it didn't get better than this for a woman, did it? She'd won the ultimate prize, and if she didn't know how to enjoy it, that was her problem.

"Do you remember the day we met?" he asked.

Alice did not. She'd been blackout drunk at the time, but she knew how to hold her liquor, so he hadn't been able to tell. In the last two years, though, he'd told this story enough that she'd been able to piece together a fabricated memory of it. So she said, "Yes, how could I ever forget?"

He laughed. "Sometimes I think about how lucky it was, you know? My first visit to the livestock rodeo, and I meet the woman of my dreams. I'd begged Travis not to drag me along, too." He rubbed a thumb over the back of her left hand. "Who'd have thought I'd fall for the runner-up of the pig-wrestling competition?"

"Runner-up my ass. I was robbed. Jean Anne's pig was hardly greased up at all. Should've been an automatic DQ." It was the only bit of that day she remembered, a shard of a memory that had lodged itself, against all odds, in her mind. She'd yelled at the officials until someone—she couldn't remember exactly who—had grabbed her and pulled her away. She couldn't deny that pig wrestling got her worked up.

That was why she did it.

Well, not anymore. Her pig-wrestling days were over now. This restaurant made that clear enough. So did the dress. She felt feminine, which was something she hadn't even considered growing up as the youngest with six older brothers. None of them could wrestle a hog like she could, though. Talk about a Luck family claim to fame. "You were born for it," her father often said, and she took it as a compliment every time. It was the only one he ever offered.

Jacob squeezed her hands in his. "I've never met anyone like you, Alice. You blow me away. You inspire me to try new things. You turn me on constantly. All I want to do is make you happy."

Their waiter dropped off two drink flutes, and Alice stared at them, confused. Her first thought was: *This isn't how you serve up a jalapeño margarita.* And her second thought was: *Aw hell.*

The ring glimmered among the bubbles at the bottom of the champagne flute.

He was down on one knee so fast, he might have fallen out of his chair. Still clutching her hand, he began the spiel that she now realized he'd begun prior to the arrival of the ring. But she hadn't seen it. She'd been thinking about greased-up pigs instead.

"Alice Louisa Olivia Luck—"

She jerked her head back. "Olivia?"

"Yeah, it's on your birth certificate."

"No, it's not."

"Yes, it is. I double-checked."

"Ah. Alright, then."

"Alice Louisa Olivia Luck, I've loved you since the moment I met you. You fascinate me, inspire me, and I crave you like no one I've ever met. All I want to do is take care of you every day for the rest of our lives, to fulfill your every need, to provide for you, to love you, to make love to you, and to build a beautiful family with you. Would you do me the honor of marrying me?" He grabbed the champagne flute, quickly downed the liquid, and dumped out the ring. The emerald at the center of the diamond-studded band shone like a star under the rooftop's string lighting.

He'd matched not only the dress but the ring to her eyes.

Everything was perfect. He'd created a dream proposal, taken care of every detail, and designed it all around her.

She was the centerpiece of this night.

This was an easy decision. She was into men, and she wouldn't do better than Jacob on that front. If she'd learned anything in college, it was that.

This could be great. All she had to do was say yes. Her

beautiful life was laid out before her, everything tailored to her needs.

She beamed down at the gleaming emerald.

Wait.

Had he said he wanted to start a family with her? They'd never discussed kids.

And then her mind flashed to the radical redshift permanent marker, which she'd brought along for reasons unknown in her handbag.

The whole restaurant was staring at them now.

"Jacob, I love you, I do."

He knew immediately and bowed his head.

Cringing, she leaned closer and whispered, "Should I say yes right now and then we can go over it later?"

"No, Alice." He deposited the ring in the inside pocket of his jacket as he found his seat again. She avoided the judgment of the onlookers by turning her attention toward the table.

"I'm sorry," she whispered. "I don't know if I'm ready yet."

"Typical."

The word felt like a slap, and she jerked her head back. Was Jacob being ... critical? Of her?

"What do you mean, *typical*? What the hell's that supposed to mean?"

"What do you think it means, Alice? Jesus. I give you everything you could ever want. What more is there that I don't give you? What are you waiting for? Dammit, I should've known." He downed the second flute of champagne. "You're the biggest flake I've ever met. You can't even hold down a job."

Oh, he wanted a fight? Right now? Perfect. He'd deprived her of the opportunity for years with all his kindness and understanding. They were overdue.

"Bull," she said. "I just got my degree two months ago, and the job market's hard." She clenched her fists in her lap. She didn't want to hit him, but mostly she did want to hit him, and perhaps in a few parallel realities, she went for it.

But not this one.

Instead, she hissed through gritted teeth, "I didn't go to school for eight years to be called a flake."

"Why did it take you eight years to get your bachelor's degree, then? You couldn't stick to a major. How many times did you change?"

"We've talked about this, Jacob. I'm a renaissance woman."

"Stop saying that. Taking medieval studies as an elective doesn't make you a renaissance woman. It's not even the same era."

"I have to sample things before I can pick the right one. That doesn't make me a flake. It makes me thoughtful!"

Alice had carried on drunken conversations with ice sculptures giving off more warmth than Jacob was now. "Is that what this is?" he said. "You're saying you haven't sampled enough men?"

"No! That's not what I'm saying. I've sampled plenty of men."

"Plenty? What am I, item number twelve on the menu?"

She almost laughed at the lowball guess, but now wasn't the time. "I still want to be with you, Jacob, it's not—"

He held up a hand. "Please stop. Stop. I should've seen this coming. All my friends warned me this would happen—"

"The hell? Which friends?"

"They said you'd run at the first sign of something

stable. I didn't want to believe them, but they were obviously right."

"I don't run from stability."

"You've never let me in, Alice."

"Says the man who picked out my period panties. How much closer do you need to be, Jacob? Wanna chart my cervical mucus?"

"I wouldn't have to track everything you do if you'd tell me what was going on inside you, let me in. I feel like you're this safe I can't crack. I don't know what's in there, and all I can do is knock on it or scan it with some infrared to guess what's inside. So that's what I do. I spend all day trying to break into the damn safe!"

"I let you inside plenty! You know all about me. You call my mom Patty."

"Yes, and Patty is a lovely, open woman."

"She's a sexually repressed zealot, and you know it."

The waiter had been on his way back to the happy couple and was only five feet from the table when Alice mentioned her mother. Smartly, he turned and walked the other direction.

"Last time we visited," Jacob replied, "when you were out shooting with Kyle, Patty and I had coffee together, and she opened up to me more than you ever have." He was pointing now, jabbing a finger at her with each new accusation. "She told me about her deepest fears."

Alice rolled her eyes. "You mean the End Times?"

"Well, sure. But it isn't about what she fears that matters —it's about trusting me enough to tell me about it."

"She tells *everyone* about the End Times, Jacob! She won't shut up about it!" Alice fought the urge to stand and leave, but the urge was strong. Walking away would only prove Jacob's point, though, so she pressed her backside more firmly into her seat. "I don't know what you want from me. You know everything a person could about me. If that's not enough for you, then I'm not enough for you."

He opened his mouth but only shook his head and leaned back in his seat, snapping the wormhole of rage between them. "What are you afraid of, Alice? I honestly don't know."

"I'm not afraid of anything."

"Then how come you look like you're about to sprint out of here?"

"I'm not fixing to sprint out of here." She wadded up the napkin from her lap and threw it on the table.

"Then should we order an appetizer?"

It was a direct challenge, and she'd never backed down from one of these in her whole life. It was how she'd ended up doing donuts on an ATV in the sheriff's front yard when she was only thirteen years old. She'd felt bad running over his garden gnomes in the process, but it hadn't been her fault; Tommy never should've said she wouldn't do it.

She met Jacob's stare. "I think the calamari looks delicious."

"Do you know what that is?"

"Yes," she said, "it's squid. Please. I'm not completely uncultured." *Thank you, Intro to Marine Biology.*

"Okay, then." He searched around then flagged down the waiter. "If you're not going to run—"

"I'm not."

"—let's get the calamari."

"Let's do it."

And that was when the spacecraft appeared out of the night sky.

It was not there one second, then *zup*, it was there. The diameter of two pickup trucks, it hovered at the level of the rooftop, twenty feet above the bustle of East Seventh. But shouts of terror didn't erupt from below.

The exterior of the craft shimmered like the night sky, and from Alice's point of view, it was easy enough to pick out, as it blocked the lights and view of the bars across the road.

She wasn't the only one on the rooftop with the right viewing angle.

"Oh my God!" another diner shouted.

Jacob gasped. "Alice, get down!" He reached for her arm, but she slipped from his grasp. He went to the ground without her.

When a hatch opened, Alice wasn't entirely surprised to see Liz Windsor standing at the threshold.

"Congratulations, Miss Luck. The position is yours. I believe you said you could start immediately?" Her eyes traveled to Jacob. "Oh dear, I am ever so sorry! Am I interrupting something?"

"Yes!" snapped Jacob, poking his head above the table enough to glare at the new arrival. "What the hell is this? Who the hell are you?"

Alice grabbed her handbag from the back of her chair. "This is Liz Windsor. She interviewed me today. I guess I got the job."

Jacob's mouth hung open until he managed to say, "What's the job?"

Alice turned to her rescuer. "Yeah, what's the job? Actually. Doesn't matter. That's a spaceship, right? How do I get in? Do I jump, or ...?"

A bridge shot out from the open hatch, landing on the rooftop patio, and Alice didn't hesitate to climb up onto the ledge. To her credit, she hesitated before crossing, looking back at her dinner companion. "Sorry, Jacob. I, uh, I really need a job."

She didn't wait for a response, just scooted across the metal plank.

As she stepped past Liz Windsor and before the hatch shut behind her, she swore she heard Jacob say, "Typical."

CHAPTER
THREE

"Where are we going?" Alice asked, not especially caring where, so long as it wasn't back to Vive and the proposal blow-up she'd narrowly escaped.

"To headquarters."

The interior of the spaceship looked more like the party buses Alice had frequented in her time at Texas A&M than it did anything particularly high tech. She couldn't see a control panel or anything like it. Instead, padded cream-colored seats, on which Alice had already made herself quite comfortable, ringed the outer walls of the circular space. "What's with the stripper pole?" she asked, pointing to the metal rod in the center.

"Sometimes the DeepShuttles can get a little crowded, and those who must stand need something to hold on to."

"A DeepShuttle? Is that what this is called?"

"Ah, yes." Liz Windsor ran her hands down the tops of her legs, smoothing out the fabric of her leg-hugging skirt. "I forget that most Homo sapiens are unfamiliar with what so many of us take for granted."

"Hold up. You separated yourself out from Homo

sapiens. Does that mean you're not one?" The spaceship was, of course, a massive contextual clue.

"I am not," Liz Windsor confirmed. "I used to be, but I've been almost entirely reconstructed. You see, I was crushed nearly to death by a malfunctioning DeepShuttle."

Alice cringed and searched for something to brace herself on, but only found more of the seat next to her. She didn't feel like touching the stripper pole.

"I don't remember the accident," Liz Windsor explained, as if that helped. "But because the Depot was at fault, they paid for my reconstructive surgery, offered me gainful employment, and my life has been better for it." She smiled. "The Depot takes care of their people."

"When you say the Depot … are we talking Paper Depot?" Alice's brain struggled to reconcile everything she was currently experiencing with an office supply store that still had an aisle for fax machines.

"Not *exactly*. The Depot is— Well, you'll begin to understand soon enough."

Alice accepted that for now and returned to her original question. "So, where are we going?"

"The same place where you interviewed."

"The Paper Depot?"

"Yes."

Alice could see herself getting bored of this conversation quickly. "How much longer till we're there?"

Liz Windsor stood. "Oh, we've been there. Here. Almost since the moment I closed the hatch behind you. I thought you might like a little time to sit down and gather yourself after the sudden departure. But if you're ready to get started, I would love to introduce you to the rest of your crew."

"Crew? What is the job again?"

"We'll get to that in good time." The hatch opened, and Liz Windsor stepped out onto the plank. "Follow me."

Alice did, because she was already fairly committed to this mystery now, and found herself in a large hangar.

"No use screaming for help," Liz Windsor said. "We're underground. No one will hear."

Alice whipped her head toward the woman. "Why would I scream for help?"

"I haven't a clue. You're not in any danger at the moment. But people do the strangest things sometimes."

Only once they rounded the side of the craft they'd ridden in on did Alice realize that it wasn't the only one in the cavernous space. She caught a glimpse of a chrome behemoth on the other end of the hangar right before Liz Windsor led her through a heavy door and into a sterile hallway. At the end was a set of stairs leading up. It was the same hallway she'd visited earlier that day for the interview.

They didn't enter the interview room, but rather took another door that opened into yet another hallway. Alice began to grow suspicious that there might be an entire catacomb of sterile hallways in this complex below the office supply store.

This must be a government job, then. Something with the CIA? Or perhaps NASA would make more sense. Did the CIA have a NASA division? Surely it must, what with all the billionaires throwing their hands into the space race lately.

When they finally left the hallway and stepped into one of the rooms, Alice felt tremendously overdressed.

They'd entered a lounge, complete with sofas, a four-seater table, and a long coffee bar that, based on the lingering aroma, had recently been used.

She almost didn't notice the figure standing with her

back to the door on the other side of the room, that was how still the woman was. She seemed to be inspecting a painting on the wall.

"Enjoying the artwork, Miss Machiavelli?" asked Liz Windsor.

As the stranger turned, Alice wondered if she'd ever encountered anyone so immediately intimidating. This woman was tall, lean, and had a nose made for cutting diamonds while turning it up at people with lesser noses. Her dark hair was in an immaculate French braid that ran perfectly down the center of her head and draped over one shoulder and down past her breasts.

The most devastating part was that the woman's garb was that of some strange elfin warrior, which should have made *her* look like the freak, but only made Alice feel like a delicate flower in her flowing emerald dress. At least she'd opted for boots over heels.

Miss Machiavelli, as Liz Windsor had addressed her, also wore boots, but hers matched the rest of the leatherwork of her ensemble.

The warrior woman set down the coffee mug on the nearest flat surface without sparing it another glance and marched over to Alice and Liz Windsor.

"The strokes could be more precise," Miss Machiavelli replied without a trace of humor. She paused only a few feet from the other women and looked down her nose at Alice as she waited to be formally introduced.

"Miss Luck, this is Susy Machiavelli. Miss Machiavelli, this is Alice Luck."

"Call me Vel, please." The women shook hands, and Alice was ready. She'd sized up Susy in a heartbeat. You didn't attend dozens of livestock shows and rodeos without learning to spot a hand crusher from a mile away.

She met the other woman's grip pound-per-square-inch by pound-per-square-inch and tried not to let her satisfaction show as Vel's right eyebrow hitched up almost imperceptibly with surprise.

"I had expected the ship's help to be dressed … differently," Vel said, scanning Alice from top to bottom.

"Oh, no," Liz Windsor replied, almost giggling. "The ship will be staffed minimally for this mission. But I think you'll find the operating system will easily handle all of your essential needs. Miss Luck here is your captain on this voyage."

"Voyage?" Alice said.

"*Captain?*" said Vel.

Liz Windsor smiled politely. "Miss Luck—well, Captain Luck—will lead the trial mission."

"You're kidding me," said the other two, though in markedly different tones.

"No, not at all. Captain Luck, meet your second-in-command. I have full faith that Lieutenant Machiavelli will serve you well on your mission."

Alice stood a little taller in her boots as she grinned at the lieutenant. *Her* lieutenant. "Well, I'll be damned, Susy. Looks like you and me are gonna be thick as thieves."

Vel's top lip curled almost imperceptibly. "Vel, please. No one calls me Susy."

"For real?" Alice said. "No one? That's a shame."

Liz Windsor's laugh sounded unnatural but not disingenuous. "Getting along already! We do take personality very much into account when we hire on a new crew. Once we've completed our personality assessments, we run them through a harmony algorithm that ensures the odds of onboard murder among crew members do not exceed fifty percent."

"So it's not a complete coin toss," Alice said. "That's good to know. Sounds like quite the algorithm." What little she knew about algorithms she'd learned in her calculus class, and, even still, she was confusing the term with "logarithm," which she equally didn't understand. "Always important to have a strong one of those."

"Indeed," said Liz Windsor, then she motioned to a pair of couches facing one another, and Alice was happy enough to take a seat. But while Vel approached the other one, she didn't sit. "I prefer to stand, if that's all right."

Alice turned to Liz Windsor, who had taken a seat beside her. "As captain, what happens when I give an order?"

"Your crew must follow it."

"Have a seat, Susy." Alice searched for signs of insubordination, but all she found was a small, twitching muscle in the lieutenant's jaw. "Yes, Captain." Then she sat.

Liz Windsor proceeded like she hadn't noticed a thing. "I think you'll find that Lieutenant Machiavelli is exactly the sort of second-in-command you'd want on your first trip out. She's been awarded the Crab Nebula's highest honor of Bloodthirsty Renegade three times, finished first in her Defensive Mass Slaughter training with the Depot, and has nearly encyclopedic knowledge of the quanta of the universe."

"Eh," Alice said, "she'll do, I suppose. Wait, how does she have all that stuff? I thought Homo sapiens—"

"I'm not a Homo sapiens," Vel replied.

Alice looked from one person to another for an explanation. Vel certainly looked like a human being.

Liz Windsor was happy to explain. "Lieutenant Machiavelli is a parallel being."

"Ah, of course," said Alice. "How could I have missed it?"

Vel narrowed her eyes at her captain. "You have no idea what that is, do you? I'm from a parallel universe."

"Duh," said Alice. "What else could it mean?"

Liz Windsor giggled. "Of course! What else could it mean? Really, Lieutenant Machiavelli, you think we would hire on someone so unfamiliar with the basics of infinite worlds theory?"

"Hah," said Alice, "right? No way."

"And Lieutenant Machiavelli, I'm not sure if you've caught on to this yet, but Captain Luck is a *native Texan.*"

Alice wondered only briefly how that claim to fame stacked up against the Crab Nebula's award before she decided to stop worrying about it and instead really drive the privilege home. "Eighth-generation Texan."

Liz Windsor gasped, and even Vel couldn't hide the subtle sliver of jealousy that passed like a shadow across her expression.

"I had no idea about *all that,*" Liz Windsor breathed. "I feel even better about our selection now!"

Alice, who had given up on following the logic of this conversation as soon as the words "parallel being" entered it, smiled and kicked her Texas-flag boots up onto the coffee table in front of her. She knew praise when she heard it, at least, and the title of Captain Luck was starting to grow on her.

As far as she could tell, she would be manning a ship of some kind, very likely a spaceship, judging by the obvious clue provided by the hangar, and she would be respected and have a fully capable second-in-command who could figure out whatever nagging details came along.

This wasn't a bad first job out of college. Better than extracting semen from turkeys, which was, according to her degree, about the best she could've reasonably hoped for.

As long as there were no turkeys in space, she would be fine.

"It's not that I have anything against turkeys," she said, "but what is this job again? And does it involve turkey semen?"

Liz Windsor, who had not been privy to any of the happenings within Alice's mind that had led up to the statement on turkeys, arched her eyebrows, but addressed the question. "No turkey semen, Captain, and I'll provide the full briefing once the remaining new member of the crew arrives. I believe he's due here in a few—"

There was a knock at the door before it opened. The bland-faced Mike from her interview grinned as he walked in, his expression both annoyingly readable and vacant. "Hello, ladies. Minister Zone has arrived by transport. Are you ready for him?"

"Oh!" Liz Windsor clapped excitedly. "Yes! He's a few minutes early, but do let him in! I'm so excited to introduce him to the crew." She was already on her feet, and Vel and Alice followed suit. And then the strangest being Alice had ever seen walked into the room, clutching a steaming chalice in his armored hand.

"Oh dang," he said, frowning. "If I'd known there was coffee here, I wouldn't have brought my own from the ship. Blast. I hate to be wasteful."

Liz Windsor rushed over to greet the newcomer, but Alice, usually the *first* to chase after anything resembling an armadillo, hung back.

And that was about what he looked like—a human armadillo. The skin on his arms was a smoky, pearlescent plated armor that seemed to bend and move easy enough as he shook Liz Windsor's hand. Each plate was small enough that the edges didn't appear to snag any of the clothes he wore over them—in this case, wide-legged jeans and a Nirvana T-shirt with Kurt Cobain's head ironed on below the band name.

The creature lacked hair on his head, which Alice was immediately relieved about once she tried to imagine what he would look like with it. His face was the only unarmored place on his body that she could see, though it was anyone's guess what was happening underneath those JNCOs. She decided not to guess.

The skin of his face was the same color as the scales, but it *was* skin, or something that looked close to it in elasticity. He had two almond eyes, a nose like a molehill, and a thin-lipped mouth that wouldn't stop bumbling on about the coffee mix-up.

"I'm happy to make you a cup," Liz Windsor announced, clearly enamored. "But first, allow me to introduce you to your captain and lieutenant!"

He followed Liz Windsor over to the couches, and it was Vel who had the sense, and the courage, to step forward and offer her hand.

The armadillo man wiped a sweaty palm on his jeans before taking the lieutenant's, and Alice saw that he could only meet Vel's eyes for a millisecond before looking away.

"That is your lieutenant, Susy Machiavelli, and this is your captain, Alice Luck. Lieutenant Machiavelli and Captain Luck, this is Dan Zone, who we've contracted out from the Ministry of Weapons and Culture."

"Howdy," Alice said, taking a steadying breath before offering her hand.

"Wow," Dan said, and unlike when he shook Vel's hand, he seemed unable to take his eyes off Alice's face.

"I know," Liz Windsor said, sounding giddy. "She's the

real deal." Then, "Mike, would you make fresh coffee for us while we chat?"

Alice had almost forgotten about good ol' Mike, who'd been hovering by the door.

"Absolutely, Liz Windsor!"

As he set out to work, the other four settled in on the sofas. Alice found herself next to Vel and quickly gave the lieutenant as much space as she could before returning her attention to Liz Windsor.

"Minister Zone is originally from Pangoliarch, correct?" Liz Windsor asked. He nodded. "A Very Fine Planet. Well respected. Cautious. With his vast knowledge of the universe's many unique cultures and weaponry, Minister Zone will be in charge of risk assessment for your crew. While you will ultimately make the decisions that matter, Captain Luck, I hope that you'll defer to Minister Zone's judgment as often as possible. He is among the best at what he does."

"Weapons and culture?" asked Alice. "Are those, like, two different divisions?"

Dan cocked his head to the side. "No. Why would they be?"

"That's not how they do it on Earth."

"It's not?" replied Dan.

Alice thought it over. "No, I guess it *is* how they've done it here, more or less."

Mike brought over fresh coffee, and Alice accepted gladly, despite the late hour. She cradled it in her hand and leaned against the armrest. "So, we're going to space, right?"

Liz Windsor grinned. "Outer."

"And we're doing that in a spaceship, yeah?"

Dan caught Vel's eye and whispered, "She did say *Luck* was the captain, right? Not you?"

Alice heard the shade but ignored it. She didn't know what being a Texan qualified her to do in space, but it was clearly not nothing. In other words, she felt her job was secure enough to ask a few dumb questions. "So, who will be in charge of steering the ship?"

Vel emitted a stifled grunt from deep in her gut, and Dan's eyes darted nervously between Liz Windsor and Alice.

Liz Windsor's cheery smile faltered. "Well, no one. The operating system navigates and steers, so—"

Alice was well aware that she'd lived a sheltered life. She'd learned that in heaps when she'd moved from Slip'n'fall, Texas, population 147, to College Station. Everyone knew more about the world than she did there. And she learned it again when she moved from College Station, population tens of thousands of drunk college students, to Austin.

Those pivotal moves had taught her an important skill: recognizing when her ass was showing.

Now was one of those times. So, she interrupted Liz Windsor, "I'm kidding, I'm kidding. Trying to lighten the tension. Y'all thought I believed it worked like some old pirate ship with a big wooden wheel or something? Ha!"

Liz Windsor guffawed, and Dan chuckled reservedly. Vel didn't laugh, and Alice had the sneaking suspicion that the woman knew none of it had been a joke.

Vel had caught a glimpse of Alice's ass, so to speak, and wasn't going to be convinced she hadn't.

Mike was the last one to stop laughing, and he shut it off like someone had taken a machete and hacked clean through the mirth.

Liz Windsor made to wipe away a tear, though Alice

could see no wetness glimmering on the woman's smooth cheeks. "Woo, I tell you. If I could join you on this mission, I would. I know it's going to be full of laughter and joy and adventure and camaraderie."

"I have a good feeling about it, too," Alice muttered, arching a brow at Vel, who was visibly clenching her jaw. "What's wrong, Susy? You can't wait to get started?"

"Speaking of getting started," Liz Windsor said, slapping her knees. "How about I brief you on the mission? Mike, bring over the projector, please!"

He did as he was told, rolling over a small table with a concave surface. It jumped to life with a flash, and Alice was treated to a hovering hologram of a bumpy orb. How exciting, she thought. *Just like in the movies.*

"You three," Liz Windsor said, "have been recruited to the Depot's elite DeepService Team One."

Alice was sure to *ahh* along with the other two.

"Our clients appreciate our complete discretion, since, as you've probably guessed, hiring us requires them to first admit they have reproductively failed as a species. Admitting one's own infertility issues can be hard enough for many. Admitting that your entire apex species has somehow managed to make itself impotent is another matter entirely. As I'm sure you know, Alice, from your topnotch education, when an entire species fails to procreate with any meaningful regularity, it is usually not nature that has caused such a thing."

"Like the turkey!" Alice said.

Liz Windsor and Vel both jerked their heads back in a rather turkey-like fashion.

"Hold on ..." Liz Windsor said, eyeing Alice closely, but not without a clear sense of pride.

"Oh no," Vel muttered. "Did she know ... Is she a genius?"

"Yes," Alice said, folding her arms across her chest. "Yes, I am. But why do you ask?"

Liz Windsor said, "You mentioned the turkey earlier. You'd already projected ahead, hadn't you?"

Alice leaned back, clasping her hands behind her head. "Ah, dang. I was hoping you wouldn't figure that out about me yet. Carry on."

Dan gasped. "She did it again," he said to Liz Windsor. Then, to Alice, "What a pun!"

Good hell, she was lost. "Ah, yeah, well. I do love a good pun. Smart of you to get it. You, uh, care to explain it to the others?"

"Carry on. It's a play on the word 'carrion,' which is a classification of Blerg VFP69 birds. And the most well-known carrion bird in this region of the planet is ... the *turkey* vulture."

Liz Windsor's hand flew up to her mouth, and Vel said, "Holy quasar. Are you kidding me? I could've sworn she was an imbecile."

Alice chuckled. "You wish."

"I don't wish," Vel said earnestly. "You're my captain. I don't want an imbecilic captain."

"Right. Of course not." Alice decided to stop speaking while she was ahead. She'd spent her life being told she was better off when she didn't speak—first from her family, then a string of almost boyfriends, and even a few professors. This was the first time she could recall that anyone had mistaken her for a genius, and she was at least smart enough to know she shouldn't push it.

"The planet you will be visiting," Liz Windsor continued—

and it took all the restraint Alice could muster not to shout, *"Planet?! We're going to a different planet?"*—"is Graug VFP3867, known locally as Bacc'nalia. Queen Phet has enlisted our help, as the birth rate among her people has dropped significantly in the last hundred Bacc'nali years and is expected to reach zero within two generations. You will be sent out on a trial basis. If you succeed in finding a suitable genetic match for the Bacc'nali people during the allotted time frame, you will be rewarded with a yearlong contract from the Depot. You will officially become the new DeepService Team One."

"Timeout," Alice said, tapping the fingertips of one hand into the palm of the other. "Are you telling me I've been hired as a *matchmaker?*" The only matchmaking she'd ever done was between her friends Tricia and Kenny, freshman year of college, and while it had technically led to sparks, not all sparks were created equal; some sparks were, by the campus police standards at least, "domestic violence."

Tricia had served fifteen months for Alice's fancy bit of matchmaking, and Kenny ... well, she hoped he was doing all right wherever he'd ended up after the name change.

Liz Windsor laughed good-naturedly at the question. "Matchmaking! I suppose it *is* a bit like that. Except we're more concerned with the biological side of it. Perhaps *husbandry* is a better term for it. That's why you're the captain, after all."

"Alien husbandry?" Alice looked at the others to see if they were as shocked as she was. Or maybe this was some practical joke.

But neither Vel nor Dan seemed especially amused by the concept.

"Okay, then. Sounds fun." She scooted closer to Vel on the couch and threw an arm around the woman's shoulder. It was like hugging a statue. "Looks like the three of us are going to become best friends. You, Dan, with your knowledge of weapons and culture, me with my vast, genius-level knowledge of animal husbandry, and Susy with her Crab awards and ability to set the mood through steely glares alone."

"There is one more member of the crew," Liz Windsor added. "Caid Sonorian. He is a universally certified mental health facilitator who, I assure you, is the best there is for helping a crew such as yours with the many inevitable traumas found in this line of work."

Alice tilted an ear toward Liz Windsor. "The whats?"

"Don't worry. Like I said, Caid will be there to help. I asked him to join us, but he said he'd prefer to get on board early and meditate to mentally prepare. You'll meet him shortly, and I believe you'll all get along great. He has a natural ability to meet his clients exactly where they are. Honestly, I'm shocked that we were able to hire him on again. He's usually in high demand."

Alice kept her arm around Vel as she asked the woman, "You ever been to a shrink?"

"I'm not sure what you mean."

"A head doctor."

"Yes, I have." Vel said it with not the slightest hint of shame that Alice thought one ought to have.

She let go of the woman's shoulders and gave her some space. "I guess your home universe isn't *quite* parallel to this one, then." She addressed Liz Windsor. "I assume the mental health counseling is voluntary."

"Not entirely. An initial assessment is required for the position. After that, it's up to you and Caid to decide how frequently you meet in an official and confidential capacity. However, if you fail to adhere to his recommendations, it is considered grounds for termination."

"That hardly seems fair," said Alice.

"It may not seem fair to you, but trust me when I say it's the only fair thing for the rest of the crew."

Alice held up her hands in surrender. "Fine, fine. Back to the mission. We gotta find a booty call for the Bachnes?"

"Bacc'nalis. Yes. The onboard operating system will assist you in this, as will Minister Zone's cultural expertise. You'll have access to an onboard database that is searchable, but of course, one must know what to search for. And that is where your qualifications come into play, Captain Luck." Liz Windsor leaned toward Dan and whispered, "She earned a grade point average of 2.4 out of 2.4. I *do* wish I could be there to watch her in action." A longing sigh, then: "Plenty more information awaits you all aboard your ship, and you'll also have means of communicating with me during your mission. I will serve as your official liaison with the Depot. You'll have forty-eight hours of ship time to not only decide upon a suitable match for the Bacc'nalis, but also have Queen Phet and the dignitary in charge of the compatible race sign the formal agreement of interbreeding. If you can complete the mission in that time frame, then the yearlong contract is yours, along with the salary."

"And if we don't?" Alice asked. "Time to kick rocks?"

"I'm not familiar with that delightful expression, but if it means you will be unable to return to Blerg VFP69 —I mean, *Earth*—and will instead be banished to one of the outer planets to live out the rest of your days, then yes, you will 'kick rocks.' It's nothing personal. We can't risk your telling Depot secrets throughout the multiverse once you are no longer under temporary contract." (Liz Windsor's cheerful grin only served to confuse Alice.) The liaison's head hitched to the side, and she laughed. "I suppose that works! The outer planets are barren wastelands made almost entirely of dry rocks. So, yes, you could kick said rocks for entertainment!"

Dan began wringing his hands, and he scanned the room for an exit.

"When you say banished," Alice said, "I mean, it sounds like probably not a good thing, but then you're smiling, so …"

Liz Windsor's head tilted to the side. "Oh, I apologize for the confusion. I'm smiling because I have full faith that a crew this talented is at no risk of failure."

"But if we do, you'll banish us."

Liz Windsor chuckled. "Of course not."

Dan laughed nervously. "Of course not, Captain Luck. Why would someone—"

"That unpleasant task would be left to Mike," Liz Windsor concluded. "He would input the coordinates to the ship and send you off to exile."

Mike, who had taken a seat in the far corner of the room, grinned and waved when Alice snapped her attention to him.

"Mike will condemn us to a barren wasteland if we don't find a suitable match for the Bacc'nalis?" Alice turned to Vel. "Are you hearing this, Susy?"

"It sounds like you're not used to threats," Vel said. Then, to Liz Windsor: "You're *sure* she's supposed to be the captain?"

Feeling a need to defend her honor, Alice said, "Look at Dan! He's not used to it either."

Dan Zone's armored skin glistened with something not unlike perspiration as he said, "Oh, I'm used to it. People threaten me all the time. Part of being in the Ministry of Weapons and Culture."

"Look at you, man," Alice said, "you're a nervous wreck. You're *not* used to it."

"I'm used to getting threats *and* being a nervous wreck. I don't see why the two must be mutually exclusive."

"Besides," Vel added, "he's not our *captain*. He doesn't need to be brave."

"Oh please," Alice said, "I'm brave. Have *you* ever taken on a family of wild hogs with nothing but a bowie knife because you forgot your hunting rifle at Esteban's house when you made your early-morning escape and decided to cut through the Steinbacher property so your nosy neighbor Kennedy Payne wouldn't see you on your walk of shame?"

"That's very specific," said Vel, "so, no."

"Ah, well, uh ..." Alice looked around. "Neither have I. But I expect I would show a lot of courage in that situation, especially if I ended up with a nasty scar down my calf because I let one of the adolescent hogs sneak up from the rear."

Vel's eyes darted down the exposed portion of Alice's legs, and Alice quickly tucked her right shin behind her left. "The point is, I'm courageous."

"Of course you are!" Liz Windsor said. "Which is why I have no doubt in my mind that this will be the best DeepService Team One we've ever had. Now, how about we tour the transit?"

CHAPTER
FOUR

Liz Windsor's kitten heels tapped across the concrete floors as the group emerged into the vast underground hangar. Alice hurried to catch up. "What's the deal with the Bacc'nalis, exactly? Is it infertility, or ...?"

"That's for you to figure out, Captain Luck. They're not sure what it is, but Queen Phet has made it sound like their dwindling reproduction is not for lack of trying. I'm sure you've come across plenty of infertility in your formal education."

"Of course, of course." Alice refrained from mentioning that the treatment for infertility in livestock was often auctioning off said animal to a meat-processing facility.

"You'll be traveling via cosmic fold," Liz Windsor explained as they rounded the DeepShuttle Alice had arrived in and approached the much larger craft. "Bacc'nalia is relatively nearby, so the trip will only take nine onboard hours, leaving you thirty-nine to complete the negotiations and any additional travel to compatible planets. I trust everyone but Captain Luck is familiar with this model of ship," she continued. "It is, of course, a standard DeepCUT."

Alice paused, trying to take in the sheer size of the thing. From the end of one thruster (if that was what it was) to the other was easily a football field's length, end zone to end zone.

There was something oddly familiar about the structure of it, but damned if she could figure it out. The main body of the ship, between the two probably-thrusters that arched outward on either side, was shaped a little like a V with the point slightly rounded. And presently, the rounded point began to open, revealing its own hangar large enough to fit at least one DeepShuttle without a problem.

"Why's it called a DeepCUT?" Alice asked, following after the others toward the lowering ramp.

"It's a Depot Cosmic Utility Transit. They're incredibly reliable vehicles and have earned a five-star safety rating across cosmic folds."

"Oh, that sounds good!"

Dan leaned in. "It's out of twenty-one stars."

"This particular vessel is named *Emergence*. She's seen many fascinating wonders on her trips out." Liz Windsor patted one of the metal panels of the ship.

The ramp finished lowering, and Vel asked, "What operating system will we be using? The Fillitine 8700? Or perhaps a Paramur 9184?"

Liz Windsor looked suddenly uncomfortable. "Well, since it's a trial mission, we—well, the Depot, not me in particular—decided it best to, um, provide you with an older system. However, I feel certain you won't be at any disadvantage due to the model—the catalogues have been updated to reflect current intergalactic data—but, well, you know. Not all operating systems *cost* the same."

Vel grunted. "The Depot didn't want to shell out for the best system when they weren't sure we would return. Fair enough. So then it's, what, a Jared 5400?"

A whine slipped from Liz Windsor's mouth, like some small animal was begging to escape from her stomach. "No, not a Jared 5400."

They climbed the ramp into the DeepCUT, and a silky-smooth voice, deep yet feminine, greeted them from all sides. "Welcome," it said. "I hope you make yourself at home. It feels so incredible to have someone inside me again."

Vel stopped in her tracks and turned to face Liz Windsor. "You're kidding me. Allura 4000?"

Alice looked around for a source of the voice—a speaker, anything—but found none. It seemed to be omnipresent inside the ship.

"I'm afraid so," Liz Windsor said apologetically. "There was a liquidation sale."

"Mmm," said the disembodied ship voice. "Sounds hot."

Alice turned in a small circle. "Wait, is that …?"

Vel's jaw was clenched so tightly, it was a miracle she managed to open it enough to say, "Our onboard operating system, yes."

"Why does she sound so—what's the word—*thirsty*?"

Dan was the one to answer the question. "She was designed for a different kind of mission."

Alice narrowed her eyes, trying to pick up the hint. "A … sexy mission?"

Dan's pearlescent lips were a thin, terse line as he nodded stiffly.

"But she still has all the information and knowledge we need?" Alice asked.

Allura answered, "I know things you can't imagine in

your wildest fantasies. Whatever you need, I'm happy to give it to you however you like it."

"Huh!" said Alice. "Sounds like a nice change of pace, frankly. I don't see the problem here." She addressed the open air around them. "It's nice to meet you, Allura 4000."

"The *pleasure* is mine, but I'm happy to make it yours as well."

Oh wow, thought Alice, and for the second time that day, she remembered the stripper pole in that old party bus. "I'm Alice Luck, the captain of this new crew, and I think we'll get along just fine."

"Ooh, a captain. Would you like me to call you Daddy, Captain?"

Alice cringed. "Uh. No, that's not necessary."

"I detect you might be of the wrong gender for that. Would you prefer I call you Mommy?"

"Sweet Jesus, no!" Alice shuddered. "That's worse. Way worse."

"I understand, Captain. Tell me what you like, and I'll store that *so deep* inside my operational memory."

Alice felt her face growing hot. "Just Captain Luck, if you would. Or Alice if you're comfortable with that. Anything but Mommy."

"Confirming selection: Captain Luck, Alice, or Daddy."

Alice felt the crew's eyes on her, sizing her up. "Yeah, sure, any of those. Let's, uh, let's move on. This is getting a little weird, even for me."

Dan leaned forward and whispered, "Probably best not to use the W-word too often. It can launch her kink script."

Alice grimaced. "Can we turn this thing off?"

"I have no turn-offs," said Allura 4000, "only turn-*ons*."

"System," said Vel, "activate subservience mode."

Alice expected to hear that disembodied voice riff on *that* inappropriately, but there was no reply. Phew. "Good work, number two."

Vel appeared to enjoy the praise and stood up impossibly straighter. "Now she'll only speak when spoken directly to."

Liz Windsor clapped her hands. "Marvelous! The crew is already working together so well! Shall we continue the tour?"

The liaison led the three others toward the back of the interior port, past various smaller ships, where a glass elevator awaited them. Turning sharply on her heel, Liz Windsor extended her arms and said, "Welcome to DeepCUT *Emergence*. She's seen some amazing things in her days. She has two DeepShuttles and three smaller pods in case any of you need to branch out on your own, or if any of the planets you're visiting do not accommodate a ship this size—dense forest or craggy ground being the two most common issues. The mini transits run on an extension of the main operating system, so you can chart your route on the bridge or even in the comfort of your private chambers, and then the escape craft will take it from there."

Dan scooted up beside Alice and whispered, "Don't let the small size fool you, Captain. Those are B4Bs. They're more weapon than ship. They can condense all the cosmic radiation on their surface into a single laser beam that can fire *with accuracy* from two light-years away from the target."

Alice turned her head toward him, tucking her chin back unconsciously when she remembered what he looked like. "Why would you need to shoot something two light-years away?"

"I hope we never find out. Because while the accuracy is good, anything you can see two light-years away is *way* too big to care about a little laser beam."

Alice gave him a quick once-over. He was even stranger

looking this close up. Did he carry leprosy like the 'dillos back on her family's ranch? "Kind of a useless feature, then," she said.

"Not at all," replied Dan. "It's *fun*. That's a use."

He winked at her, and she couldn't help but grin.

He'd initially struck her as a bit of a nervous Nellie, but, if he thought high-powered weapons were fun, they'd get along. "Let's take one out and give it a try ASAP."

He grinned, exposing a row of pointed pearly whites. "As you say, Captain."

God, she *did* love being called that, even if she knew this delightful role would, like everything else in her life, eventually come crashing down around her.

However, practice made perfect, and though she considered herself too modest for bragging, she *was* getting pretty good at escaping from rubble.

Liz Windsor smacked a large green button on the wall behind her, and the glass of the elevator slid upward, allowing them entrance. "I can't wait for you to see the bridge," she gushed. "The tours are probably my favorite part of this process."

"How many times have you done this before?" Dan asked.

But before Liz Windsor could answer, the elevator had arrived and opened onto the bridge.

"Wow," said Alice. "This is luxurious." It was well-lit, with ergonomic tan chairs, glowing control panels, and floor-to-ceiling glass panes with moving schematics here and there throughout.

Alice only managed a brief scan of it before the large window at the far side captured her attention. The view wasn't spectacular at present, just the wall of the underground hangar where *Emergence* was docked, but Alice had never been short on imagination, and she could practically see the stars spreading out before her.

Which was when it finally hit her: she was going to space. *Outer* space, no less. The most interesting space there was, as far as she knew.

The area of the bridge closest to the window was all business, with control panels and knobs and levers, but the back half was set up more like a lounge. A few small machines appeared to form a kitchenette, near which sat a circular table with ample seating for the crew around it.

"While the private wings do include two small meeting rooms," Liz Windsor said, "this is the main communal space of the ship. We've found it best for the crew to spend as much time together as possible, as isolation over vast space-time can become … mentally exhausting. And since each of your species evolved to exist within groups, spending a little time with each other shouldn't be a problem."

Dan chuckled. "Yes, thanks be to Void that we don't have any hankerchucks in the crew."

"Hankerchucks?" Alice asked. "I'm not familiar."

Vel offered a succinct answer. "They tear the flesh from each other when they get too close."

"Cannibals?"

"Nah," said Vel. "For sport."

Alice narrowed her eyes. "Then how do they mate?"

"Gruesomely."

Alice turned to Liz Windsor. "We're not going to encounter any hankerchucks in this mission, right?"

Liz Windsor chuckled airily. "I certainly hope not! But if you do, Dan is the person to assist you."

"I'll make a supernova out of them," Dan said, grinning.

"Ooh!" said Alice. "We could use the B4B lasers!"

Dan jerked his head back at the suggestion. "That's way more firepower than a single hankerchuck calls for." Then, turning to Liz Windsor, he said, "I see why you appointed her captain." His tone held something not far off from reverence.

"Yes," Liz Windsor said, "I'm feeling better and better about the selection by the moment!"

Alice straightened her spine and was starting to feel pretty great about herself until her gaze landed on Vel, who was practically scowling. "What?" Alice said. "You don't approve of blowing hankerchucks to smithereens?"

Through gritted teeth, Vel replied, "I'll do whatever you command, Captain."

Alice slapped her on the back, overriding the survival instinct that warned her against it. "That's the spirit, number two."

Liz Windsor pointed toward the main control panel, where Alice spotted something not too unlike a clock but also not too like a clock. There were digits, but at that present moment, they sort of fluttered around. "Look at the time! I had hoped to be able to show each of you to your private chambers, but it seems I'd better let you get started on your voyage. I don't want to disadvantage you by keeping you on Blerg VFP69 any longer than absolutely necessary. Anyhow, your names are on each of the doors, and if you have any questions, Allura will be happy to help you out."

"I bet she will," Alice muttered.

Liz Windsor clapped her hands together in front of her. "Any final questions for me?"

Though it felt a little tacky, Alice had never let that get in her way before. "What about pay? Don't think we ever discussed it."

"Ah! Yes! I forgot about that." Liz Windsor held her hands below her chin. "Well, what do you think we should pay you?"

"Excuse me?" said Alice.

Liz Windsor spoke louder. "What do you think we should pay you?"

"No, I heard you, I just don't understand what you mean. You want me to tell you what to pay me?"

Liz Windsor looked briefly to the others, asking for a hint as to where the communication was breaking down. "Is that … is that not usually how it's done?"

Sensing an opportunity for a cash windfall but not precisely sure how best to capitalize on it, Alice replied, "Yes. That's how it's always done. I apologize for being dense. A lot's been thrown at me in the last hour. I don't know where my brain was."

Relief and compassion washed over Liz Windsor's features. "Of course. I'll make sure Allura drops you a booster once you're in your room. That should help you recuperate."

A booster sounded fun enough, even if Alice was sure Allura 4000 would deliver it with a chaser of entendre.

"Name your price, then," Liz Windsor said.

Since it seemed all but a done deal that Alice would be captain of the ship, and because she could always play it off like a joke if it went over poorly, she said, "Five million dollars."

"U.S. dollars, I presume?"

"Yes."

"Done."

Alice blinked.

Liz Windsor turned to Vel next. "And you?"

"Fourteen billion dollars."

"U.S. dollars as well?"

"Yes."

"Done."

"Hold! Up!" Alice waved to get the attention of the group. "Fourteen billion is an option?"

"It's all an option," said Liz Windsor. "That's why I gave you ... the option."

"Then I want *fifteen* billion," Alice said.

"Very well."

Alice smiled smugly at Vel, who would soon be a billion dollars poorer than her.

Liz Windsor turned to Dan, who sighed, appearing put out by the discussion. "I'll take a trillion, I guess."

"U.S. doll—"

"A *trillion?*" Alice shouted. "That's allowed?"

And now Liz Windsor didn't look so sure of herself. "Yes. I thought I'd already explained that you get to name your price."

"Yeah, but ... these are insane amounts."

"On Blerg VFP69, sure," the liaison conceded.

Alice began to understand. "Ah, but on other planets, they're not that much."

"No," said Liz Windsor. "They're still quite a lot on other planets, but you'll need a lot. Queen Phet doesn't want to work with peasants on her planet's infertility issues."

"We get paid up front, then?" Alice asked.

"Partially. Fifty percent now, the rest when you successfully complete the mission."

Alice did the math. Half of fifteen billion was still an assload. "I guess that's acceptable. But I'm raising my demand."

"Very well."

"Two trillion." She didn't miss Dan's cringe. "What, upset you're not the highest paid on the ship now?"

"No, I don't mind that. It's that once you pass one trillion, nine hundred and ninety-nine billion, nine hundred and ninety-nine million, nine hundred and ninety-nine thousand, nine hundred and ninety-nine dollars and ninety-nine cents, you bump up into the next tax bracket."

Alice, who had managed to avoid paying taxes her whole life and had no plan of starting now, frowned. Higher tax bracket meant more pressure to cough up her money. "Okay, I want one trillion and one dollars." Liz Windsor opened her mouth, but Alice cut her off. "Yes, that's U.S. dollars."

"Very well. Are we all settled up with that? Time is of the essence! Literally! Ha!"

Alice didn't get the joke. "Yes, I'm happy with it. Vel? Dan?"

Dan shrugged, and Vel said, "One trillion and two."

Alice's mouth dropped. This insubordination couldn't stand.

"Great!" Liz Windsor said. "Then I'll leave you all to it."

"Wait—" said Alice, but the liaison ignored her.

"Should you need me, you can reach me through the control monitor. For obvious space-time reasons, there will be a bit of a lag in the communication while you're in transit. Usually nothing major, but it does fluctuate as most things do. So, please plan accordingly." She made for the glass lift but paused before stepping in. "Oh! I almost forgot. Once you get settled into your chambers and refreshed with the allotted booster, each of you will need to visit Caid Sonorian for your intake interview. Merely to establish a mental baseline, nothing elaborate. Allura can direct you to his office."

A few more taps of her kitten heels across the floor, then she was in the lift, waving ta-ta.

Alice watched her go then turned to the others. "Great! Off we go, I suppose. Anyone know how to fly this thing?"

CHAPTER
FIVE

"Mmm ... yes, to the left ... Just a little farther. Almost there. Yes! Oh yes! That's it!"

Alice Luck arrived at the door with her name on it. "Thanks, Allura."

"No, thank *you*."

There was no clear handle or knob on the door to her chambers, but there was a pad with an outline of a hand on it. She pressed her palm to it, and the door slid open with a satisfying swish.

"Holy ..." Alice stepped inside the room and couldn't believe what she was seeing. "It's like a porno. But an *expensive* one." Under other circumstances, she might not have gone straight to "expensive porno" in her mind, but it was tricky not to while Allura's moans were still flip-flopping around in her brain.

In fact, while it was a nice space, it hinted at porn no more or no less than everything did.

The captain's quarters were a single airy, open space with a lush, canopied bed along one wall opposite a table and two chairs. That covered the functionality of it, at least as far as she could see. The rest was add-ons.

The wall on the far end of the room had the appearance of a bright, tropical sunset, and a hammock by it completed the look. It drew Alice to it, and she immediately ran her hand over the scene. "What is this thing?"

"It can change to look like whatever makes you feel good," Allura said. "You can change it manually, or if you'd like, I can set it to change with the overall mood of the room."

"Ooh! Do that!"

"However you like it, Daddy."

The tropical sunset was replaced by a field of bluebonnets with a few cows sprinkled around. Alice turned to the rest of the room. "Is that a hot tub?"

"Yes, it is. It can get *so hot*."

Alice turned a suspicious eye to the ceiling. "And when I'm in it, will you be watching me?"

"Only if you like an audience."

Alice considered it and decided Allura was nothing if not supportive. "Yeah, that's probably fine. We'll give it a spin, at least. Tell me about this thingy." She approached a slit in the wall by the table and chairs.

"That's your goodies slit."

"Stop."

"Which of my functions would you like me to terminate?"

"Oh, uh, none. I was speaking rhetorically, I guess. Tell me about my, uh, goodies slit."

"Anything you need to eat or drink can be ordered through that. Tell me what you want, and it'll give it to you."

"Liz Windsor mentioned a booster. Is this where I get it from?"

"It is. Would you like that?"

"Yes, please."

Not sure what to expect, Alice sidestepped, out of the path of the slit, should anything strange rocket out of it. But a split second later, there was a *ding!* and she stopped bracing herself as a small orange packet appeared in the opening. She grabbed it and held it up before tearing it at a perforated edge. What came out resembled an orange Tic Tac. "Do I just …?"

"Put it in your mouth? Yes."

"And then what happens? I get a boost?"

"Why don't you try it and find out, Captain?"

Ignoring how low-key turned on the operating system was making her feel, Alice popped the tablet into her mouth and waited. It tasted like tangerine and sunshine, and a moment after the taste registered, a warmth radiated through her body. It felt like someone had gone over her brain with a squeegee, removing all the crud from the day. A spryness overtook her muscles. "Oh wow! That's— Wow!" Then, "Oh no."

"What's got you worried, Captain? How can I ease your mind?"

"The boosters," Alice said. "These have *got* to be addictive, right? I mean, I feel better now than I would after a full night's sleep. Why would I ever sleep again?"

"If you never sleep again, you'll die." It was by far the least sexy thing the operating system had said thus far, but it still made dying sound kinda hot. "The boosters are specially designed so that every third dose that hits your system within a twenty-four-hour daylike cycle will sedate you for six hours. You'll sleep *so hard.*"

"So I only get two of these things between naps?"

"Correct. There's no chance of addiction."

"Sounds like a challenge." Alice looked around. "Do I have any clothes?"

At the question, a panel in the wall by the bed slid back to reveal a colorful wardrobe.

"Oh, this is great." Alice ran a hand over the fabrics only to realize that while the colors varied, the style of each piece did not. "Jumpsuits? Really?" She pulled a yellow one off the hanger and held it up to her, and as she did, a mirror appeared in the air opposite her. Despite that being a cool trick that she didn't understand the physics of at all, she frowned at her reflection. "I usually like a good pop of yellow, but this makes me look like a banana." As soon as she said the word, she looked around, paranoid about where Allura might take that, but the operating system said nothing.

She twisted in the mirror, trying to imagine any way that she might pull off a jumpsuit with her thick build, but none came to her. These things only looked good on tall, slender people like Vel.

She returned the yellow one to the rack. "Maybe eggplant?"

"Mmm ... I love a big, juicy eggplant."

"Christ on a pogo stick," Alice muttered. Then, remembering she was on a ship that was hurtling through space on a mission to make an alien species productively screw, she decided a little honesty was allowed. "You know what, Allura? I love a juicy eggplant from time to time, too. Yeah, purple will do for today."

CHAPTER
SIX

"Almost there," Allura 4000 whispered into Alice's ear.

Alice had to admit that the earpiece was a nice little trick. As soon as she'd stuck it in (at the prodding of the operating system), she understood the power of it. Now, she could whisper any question she wished and be the only one to hear the answer, saving her untold future embarrassment at her own ignorance of the universe.

No more stupid questions, she'd thought, but she knew that to only be wishful thinking.

"Right here. That's it. You're there."

Alice paused outside the door. Her chambers were toward the end of what she thought of as "left hall," and this one was at the far end of "right hall."

It was time for her intake evaluation with this Caid fellow. What would he look like? Would he have armor like Dan? Would he be an overachiever like Vel? And more importantly, did she knock or press a palm to the sensor and let herself in?

She opted for knocking, and a moment later, the door slid open.

A heavy draft of what smelled like lavender and coconut wafted out to meet her as she took in the room. She coughed against it, and while it wasn't an unpleasant scent, per se, she tended to prefer the earthier scents like wood smoke and manure.

The room was roughly the same size as her own chambers, and the visual wall across from the door depicted a scene from inside some sort of temple looking out over a lush green forest.

Alice became slowly aware of a deep chanting resonating through the space, as if it were a natural consequence rather than an intentional sound. There wasn't a lick of real furniture in the place—instead, the floor, which had been a sterile tiled thing in her own room, was covered in a rich woven rug of red, purple, turquoise, and gold thread generously dappled with round cushions.

Because Alice knew a little something about crossbreeding, she felt qualified to conclude that this therapy room was very likely the product of a mid-level spa having sex with a Buddhist temple.

Alice remained on the threshold, uncertain of whether she should proceed. Maybe Allura had guided her to the wrong place. Maybe this was a test pad for mating new species and the mental health assessment was actually next door.

"You must be Alice."

The man's voice was gentle but made her jump nonetheless, and she whirled to her left at the sound. Where the hell had he come from, and—

The perfect specimen of a human man stepped forward, almost making her knees buckle at the proximity.

He can't be real, can he?

"You can't be real, can you?" Alice cursed her stupid mouth as the words refused to stay inside her head.

The man smiled. "I'm Caid Sonoran. So great to meet you, Alice Luck."

Alice was no stranger to fear and arousal walking hand in hand—she'd once done the dirty with Benny Frank not fifty yards from a known rattlesnake pit—but this was a whole new level.

The man standing before her was like if someone had delved into her psyche and dredged up her wildest, most inexplicable sexual fantasies all at once. He was tall, easily six foot four, and she didn't at all mind staring up his nostrils. In fact, she loved it. She wasn't comfortable with how much she loved it, but there it was.

He wore his sun-kissed dirty-blond hair long enough to tuck behind his ears, and he stared at her with a confidence in those gray eyes that made her want to purr. His broad shoulders seemed an invitation to climb him.

She wanted to eat him, but not in a cannibalistic way. More for sport, like a hankerchuck, she supposed.

"Wow, this is great," he said.

She would chug that approval if she could. Mainline it into her veins.

He waved a palm in tiny circles in her direction. "I sense such an openness about your energy already."

Open for business, she thought. "Yeah, I guess I'm pretty relaxed all the time. I've been called a 'cool girlfriend' before."

The word "girlfriend," however, only reminded her that she'd ditched her live-in boyfriend hours before.

That sobered her up.

"Huh," he said, tilting his head to the side. "I sense a shift in you. You closed up a little."

"I—" Alice shook her head. "I don't know what I'm supposed to be doing here."

"Of course. Come on in and have a seat. There's nothing to be wary of. This is a safe space."

The door zipped shut behind her.

"I'm going to ask you to take out your earpiece, though." Caid gestured to a small divot in the wall by the door. "You can dock it here. I find we tend to have enough trouble managing our own thoughts in a coherent way without our dear, beautiful friend Allura contributing additional information. Have a seat." Caid motioned to what must be the patient cushion, a big orange drum of a pillow with a coral-colored tassel right in the center. Did she straddle the tassel? Line it up with her butthole? What was the proper position?

She chose option two and found the obstruction nestled somewhat comfortably between her butt cheeks. See? She was getting the hang of life in space already.

Caid sat cross-legged on an emerald-green cushion only a few feet away and gazed at her unblinkingly. And, in the time she'd spent deciding about the tassel, he'd grabbed an acoustic guitar and settled in with it on his lap. His right arm rested along the curves of the instrument's body while his left gently cradled the neck.

Alice whimpered. This wasn't fair. Was she really stuck on a ship with this god of a man and his guitar? There was only one way this wouldn't literally eat her up from the ovaries out: she had to sleep with him. It was unprofessional, might end up costing her a trillion dollars of lost wages, but that couldn't be helped. The sooner she slept with him, the sooner she would grow immune to his charms. Happened every time.

Granted, she'd never in her life felt this overwhelmed

and out of control around someone, but if the principle held, it held.

Caid strummed the guitar, and she struggled to keep her eyelashes from fluttering.

"Alice," he said, "you and I are going to be spending a lot of time together, so it's important that I get you know you in so much more than a professional sense. My job as the crew aide is to keep track of the emotional temperature on the ship and step in when I sense something might be causing undue stress for one of my friends. I don't expect you to trust me right away, but I hope that over time I can earn that trust."

Alice was nothing if not a quick thinker, and even in her current haze, she formulated a game plan. "I'm not generally a trusting person," she said. "If you want to earn my trust that quickly, we're going to have to spend a *lot* of time together."

Caid grinned. "Whatever it takes. Tell me, do you think of yourself as a capable person?"

"Physically, yes. I think my stamina is probably my best quality. I can hang with the best of them. Go for hours. You know, with work stuff."

"Wow, that's great." Caid strummed a lazy minor chord. "I love that you love that about yourself."

Strum ... strum, strum ...

He leaned forward. "What scares you?"

Alice struggled to think of the last time she was genuinely scared. She could think of plenty of times she probably should have been scared but hadn't been. There was that time with Old Forester's bull when it got free and caught her with her pants down, literally, out in the pasture. There was the time those douchebags from Kappa Omega convinced her to jump off the roof of their frat house into the pool that was, by all sane guesses, way too far away to be a good idea. But she'd made it. Thighs like hers were good for jumping long distances *and* sprinting away from a bull.

But it'd never been the dying that scared her. That would be quick, and then it'd be over. It was the pain before it that shook her up.

What a stupid answer, though.

She reverted to her strategy instead. "I'm scared that I'll grow old without taking full advantage of my youthful body." Would he finally get the message?

But Caid's placid expression didn't change, and the consistency of it unnerved Alice.

"I feel like you're not ready to let me in," he said.

"Oh, I am."

"Are you comfortable letting me go deeper into your mind?"

"You can go as deep as you want."

"Okay, close your eyes."

She did, trying not to grin like a greedy idiot.

"Relax. Feel the energy of the universe move through you. Because it *is* you. And you are it. We are not separate from the cosmos, but each an integral element of it. Our matter and energy are a piece of the equation of balance. We cannot be destroyed. We were a part of the All from the beginning, and we'll be here until the end ..."

Alice was beginning to think Caid wasn't going to make a move after all.

He played a low gong of a note on the guitar and let its eerie resonance wobble through the room, bounce off the walls, move through her, surround her. "I ask you again, Alice, what scares you?"

Clearly her first answer hadn't satisfied him, so she

would have to come up with something less horny. Fine. She could do that. She was a master at knowing what the teacher wanted and doing the bare minimum to reach it.

She opened her mouth to speak, but Caid cut in first. "Oh wow, interesting ..."

Alice cracked open an eye, and for the first time since she'd entered the room, Caid wasn't looking at her. He was looking at his visual wall. So, she did too.

"What?"

There was Jacob, down on one knee on the rooftop bar.

"Get out of my head! How did you even find that?"

Caid strummed his guitar again, and the scene was replaced by a mountainous landscape at sunset. "I didn't find it, Alice. You did. Your mind did. Who was that man?"

"Nobody."

"I don't believe you. *Wow*, he loves you. I mean, I could feel it, ya know?" Caid held a hand to his heart. "Does it bother you that he loves you?"

"Can't we talk about my mother or something?"

"If you like. Tell me about her."

"On second thought, no thanks. Let's talk about you. Tell me about you. What do you enjoy doing in your spare time? Are you more of a wine drinker, or do you like it a little ... harder?"

He inspected her closely. "I can't drink. Does that bother you?"

It certainly wasn't to her advantage. "Not at all. Healthy habits are great. I'm pretty healthy myself."

Caid shut his eyes softly, inhaling deeply through his nostrils and playing a few more chords on the exhale. "Mmm ... How does that make you feel?"

"What, being healthy?"

"No, the sound."

"It makes me feel … I don't know. What am I supposed to say here?"

"Relax and listen." He played it again.

And again, she felt nothing. Although … Nope, there was something. Annoyance. She was getting nowhere with him, and he seemed to be missing all the signals.

"Frequency, Alice. The course of the universe is determined by various wave frequencies. Each wave holds a set energy within it. But the remarkable thing is that sentient beings can actually *change* their frequencies. Take this guitar. I tighten the strings to achieve the sound I want to hear, the sound people expect to hear. But after enough playing, the strings start to slacken. Their frequency changes. We call that being out of tune, but who determines that? Sometimes even strings need to loosen up, and they only get that way through repeated use."

Alice was officially lost. "Yeah, that makes total sense."

Another lazy strum. "I thought you would understand. You seem like that kind of person."

"Definitely. I'm … loose." She winced. "Maybe that's not the word."

"Maybe it is. I like that word. *Loose*. It's something you'll need to keep up on this mission. Don't get too attached to your preconceived notions of the way things are. You're entering a whole new world in the truest sense. I see a resilience in you, Alice. It's going to be tested. And I'll be here for you every step of the way."

He set his guitar aside and stood, signaling the end of the session. Alice stood as well.

Caid paused by the door but didn't open it yet. "We're starting to get a feel of one another, don't you think?"

"Sure." But not before one last try. "I think it'll take more time. Maybe back in my quarters?" Yes, her mind had conjured up an image of the hot tub. It could easily fit two. She would tell him all about her mother if he would …

"I like to take people outside of their personal spaces for sessions, generally speaking."

Damn. "Right. I guess this is it for now? Should we schedule another session for later tonight, or …?"

"No need to schedule. I know where to find you. And you know where to find me." He beamed at her.

Go for it, Alice. Come on!

She lunged forward to wrap him in a hug. She couldn't take it any longer. She knew he wouldn't cross the line with her (yet), but if she didn't get that thick body up against hers, her head might explode. A hug wasn't too much to ask.

Her arms met nothing but air. She stepped back quickly. "No!" She looked up into his handsome face. "No!"

"You're disturbed. I apologize for not being clear, Alice. My body is not, technically speaking, made of matter."

"Nooo!"

Caid cocked his head to the side. "That bothers you quite a lot."

"Are you a *ghost*?"

He chuckled. "Not a ghost. An organic hologram."

"Nooo! But what about the guitar?"

"Also a hologram."

Her disappointment turned quickly to outrage. What a bait and switch!

She took a swing at him. Her fist met no resistance as it passed right through. "Dammit!"

"You're angry," he said calmly.

She slammed her palm on the pad to open the door. "And why shouldn't I be? This isn't a spaceship—this is hell!"

She snatched up her earpiece and jammed it in before stomping out the door.

"You seem hot and bothered," came Allura's voice. "What can I do to make you feel good, Daddy?"

Alice passed the entrance to the bridge and kept on walking to her wing of the ship. "Y'all got whiskey on this ship?"

"Of course."

"Then I need a shot of that and some ice-cold water in that hot tub."

CHAPTER
SEVEN

Alice's hair was still slightly damp from her ice bath as she entered the bridge and found Dan and Vel sitting at the table by the kitchenette. Neither one had changed into a jumpsuit yet, which made her feel more like a regular eggplant than a sexy eggplant, but she was also not about to change back into the emerald dress. Besides, she was captain. Captains got to be thick and purple if they wanted to be. No matter what she had on, she still knew she had better tackling form than anyone on this ship.

The tabletop was lit up with blues and reds, and as Alice moved closer, she realized they were maps and schematics.

"Caid's not coming to the team meeting, is he?" she asked.

"No," said Dan. "Why?"

"I know why," Vel replied without looking up. "He got in your head, didn't he?"

"No. This thing is a steel trap." Alice tapped at her temple.

"For what it's worth," Vel said, "I didn't enjoy my session, either."

"Wait." Dan's almond eyes grew large. "I haven't had mine yet. What happens in them?"

"My lips are sealed," Vel said, savoring the leverage.

Alice couldn't care less about that, though. "He asks you what you think your greatest strength is, then asks you what you're afraid of."

"Ah," said Dan. "That would be a short answer then a loooong answer."

"What are you afraid of, Alice?" Vel asked.

Alice took a seat at the table. "Your mom."

"My mother?"

"Yes." She paused, still not getting the reaction she'd been going for. "Never mind. I guess it doesn't translate across cultures."

"*Speaking* of cultures," Dan said, cutting in, "since the three of us are all here, we should probably get started on the brief. I've pulled all the relevant logs regarding Bacc'nali culture, so we should brief ourselves ahead of arrival. One wrong move, one mistaken gesture, and the deal could be off. Queen Phet, by all accounts, is moody. We need to anticipate that and not aggravate it."

Alice shot him the finger gun. "Gotcha. So, tell me about these people."

Dan deftly manipulated the tabletop mechanics, and an image appeared, hovering in the air between the three of them. Unlike Caid, this hologram didn't appear convincingly real. Or at all sexy.

"This is your typical Bacc'nali male, and this is your typical female."

The projected images weren't all that different from a human shape, except the proportions were all off. What passed as a torso looked more like a potato. Otherwise, the anatomy seemed straightforward. And identical between the sexes. Or maybe these were the same sex. There *was* one noticeable difference between the two examples.

"What determines whether they have two or three legs?" Alice asked.

"Huh?" Dan said. "Oh. Oh. That's not a leg."

"Holy hell. But ... where do they stick that thing?"

"A lot of places," he continued. "The Bacc'nalis aren't particular about whom they engage with in sexual intercourse—or how. There is a particular type of plant, not unlike a sycamore tree on Blerg VFP69, that they're especially fond of. It has a thick trunk that a type of rodent likes to chew a hole in at the right height to—"

Alice held up a hand. "I get it. They're not so different from Earth men after all. Better trees than livestock, I suppose."

"I see why you'd assume that, but you should know that Bacc'nalian trees scream."

Alice cringed. "Never mind, then."

"Shall I continue?" Dan asked. "Or do you have further questions about the penises?"

"Oh, I have further questions, but I guess that's more my area of expertise than yours, huh?"

Alice Luck: Penis Master. Who woulda thought?

"Supposedly, yes," Vel said, eyeing Alice with unmasked skepticism. "You *do* have a degree in this, right?"

"Not in this specifically. Afraid they don't hand out Bachelor of Dicks degrees at Texas A&M, but if they did, they'd be handing 'em out like flyers in the Quad." Her audience didn't seem to follow, and that was probably just as well. "Go on, Dan. Tell us more about the culture of this place."

"Right, right." The two- and three-legged examples continued to float above the table. Dan slipped them away, and a moment later, a banquet appeared with bodies gathered and writhing all around the foreign food and drink piled down the length of the table. "The Bacc'nalis are a festive race. They are the penultimate species on the planet insofar as conscious intelligence, and sensitive about that, so it's best not to insult their intelligence in any way."

"Penultimate?" Vel asked. "Who's the intellectually superior species?"

"A subterranean worm," Dan said, "which is not to say that the Bacc'nalis are unintelligent, just that those worms are *really pulsing smart*! You wouldn't believe the art they create with their excrement. Here. I can pull up a picture."

Alice found herself surprisingly interested in the worm shit and leaned closer to the hologram.

"Oh wow," she breathed. "That's ... gorgeous."

Even Vel seemed impressed. "The use of colors is subtle, yet it pulls me in."

As Alice tried her best to wipe a tear from her eye without anyone noticing, Dan said, "That's the point. They use their excrement artwork to lure in their prey, and then they swarm the prey from head to toe with alarming speed and latch on. Once you're covered in them, it's impossible to get them off. Someone of our size would be covered in thousands and thousands of them."

Alice felt her stomach churn. "I never trusted artists anyway." She leaned back, adding some distance between her and the hovering poop paintings. "What other terrifying dangers should we watch out for?"

"Oh, all kinds," said Dan, sounding both thrilled and terrified. "More than I could ever explain in the short time we have before arrival."

Alice snuck Vel a look to see if the lieutenant found that

as unsettling as she did, but Vel appeared strangely aroused. Danger whore. Noted.

Alice cracked her knuckles. "How about this, then, Dan? From what you know of me, what are, say, the top two ways I'm likely to step right in the shit while we're there?"

Dan accepted the challenge. "First one: if Queen Phet compliments you, it's your job to insult yourself profoundly."

"No problem. I've never taken compliments well anyway."

"Really?" Vel said. "That surprises me. I bet you get them all the time. I mean, look at you: you're smart, brave, beautiful ..."

Alice grinned. "Thanks, Vel. I think I'm pretty great t— Ah. I see what you're doing here."

Vel smirked.

"None of that," Dan said. "Let's try it again. Alice, I think you're one of the most fascinating women I've ever met."

"Thanks, Dan. I don't really know you, but the fact that you think I'm fascinating speaks highly of— Dammit!"

Vel groaned exasperatedly. "We're zapped, aren't we?"

"No!" Alice said. "Compliment me again. I'll reject it this time." She motioned for them to bring it.

Vel led the charge. "The circumference of your thighs reminds me of a warrior queen."

Alice whimpered. "Oh, but that's so *good*! Why wouldn't I accept that? Okay, fine, uh... Are you kidding me? My thighs are a sign of my peasant lifestyle, wrangling pigs in the mud like the mud person I am. A little piggy mud person."

"Good. That's good," Dan said. "And now finish by turning a compliment back to the queen."

"Meanwhile," Alice said, her mind groping wildly, "your thighs are like, um, two … pegs … of … infinite power! Yeah, like the Big Bang! They make me want to climb them like a little koala up a eucalyptus tree and nibble on your leaves."

"No," Vel said. "This is weird. And I'm baffled by how it got so weird so quickly."

So was Alice. "You do have nice legs, though, Vel."

"There!" Dan pointed at her. "Perfect! Say something *normal* like that."

"Ah, okay." Alice was starting to understand. "I guess the koala thing wouldn't have translated across planets anyway. Hey, I think we need to give Vel some practice rejecting compliments now. Vel, you have a strong command presence."

"While I don't doubt your judgment, my queen, I should tell you that all the confidence you sense in me is fake. I'm terrified all the time. My parents considered me such a failure that they exiled me to a parallel universe. You, however, command a room without even trying. It's effortless and natural, I can tell."

"Wow," said Alice. "How much of that was real? Because it felt real." She looked around. "Kinda seemed like something you should share with Caid."

Rather than responding, Vel addressed Dan. "Your knowledge of such an obscure culture as the Bacc'nalis is terribly impressive. You strike me as a smart being."

Without missing a beat, Dan replied, "Any observational skills I appear to have stem from a deep fear of the universe and a need to learn as much as I can to keep from being killed. I'm a functioning coward. Not like you, Vel."

"Sheesh," Alice said, "that was great."

Dan blinked. "What was great?"

"That … that was the exercise, right?"

"Heh." His eyes darted between the two women at the table with him. "Right. Part of the exercise. How about another survival tip?" He hurriedly pulled up a new holographic file that showed what Alice guessed was Queen Phet on her throne.

"Is that thing made of bones?" she asked.

"Yes. Now, it's important to note that while the queen enjoys a good time, she's also a certifiable psychopath." He chuckled. "I mean, we all have our quirks, right?"

Vel confirmed, "Alice wrestles pigs, I'm a decorated veteran of intergalactic wars, and the queen is a psychopath. Go on."

"Exactly. Now, you know the letter P?"

Alice crossed her arms. "I'm familiar, yes."

"You know the sound it makes?"

"Peter piper picked a … whatever," she said. "Yes, I'm good and familiar with it."

"If you use the P-sound in Queen Phet's presence, she will have you summarily executed."

"Nope," Alice said. "That can't be right."

Dan frowned. "You'd be dead right now. Bones added to her collection."

"That's insane!"

"Yes. It is. We're dealing with an insane client."

Alice felt like moping back into her room. "Some test run."

"Only the P-*sound*, though, right?" Vel asked.

"Exactly. The sound made by a 'PH' in the English language is fine. The rumor is that's some of why she hates the sound. Too many people mispronouncing her name over the years."

"We're going to be killed." Alice leaned back in her chair. "Maybe immediately."

"It's going to be tricky, no doubt," Dan said. "The key is this: talk slowly. Consider every word."

"And if we screw up?" Alice had no doubt she would. Measuring her words had never been her strong point.

Dan grinned wolfishly. "When culture fails, it's time for weapons!" He stood. "Follow me."

<hr>

Alice didn't recognize the hangar deck when the glass elevator opened up to it. The space had been transformed from only hours ago.

Holograms, she thought, taking it in. *Never thought I'd hate holograms so much.*

It looked like she'd stepped into a well-lit cave. The space itself was only half the size as before, with a holographic divider blocking her view of the loading docks for the escape pods and the port out into space. The unnerving thing was, the divider itself looked like outer space, with a view of distant stars and galaxies glittering across the blackness. But there was nothing separating her from it now. She was in it.

Dan pressed his armored hand against the holo-cave wall, and a control panel flipped out. "Here we are." He tapped a series of glowing spots on the panel, checked back over his shoulder at the wall of outer space, and said, "Ah, there we go."

Two targets made up of concentric circles had appeared, hovering over the divider.

He tapped another glowing spot, and a second panel flipped open in the cave wall.

"Ooh!" Alice said. "Guns!"

She started for them, but Vel stuck out an arm to stop her. "Blasters, technically. Why don't you let Dan train you on them first?"

"They're fairly straightforward." He picked one up off the rack. It had a short but thick barrel, and the part that Alice would usually call the cylinder looked more like the belly of a pregnant cow. "Point this end, push this button. You can line up your sights here. Just know that this *obliterates*. It's not like a Blerg VFP69 weapon that pokes a little hole in you. Only fire this when you're ready to absolutely destroy someone."

"Gimme, gimme."

"Why don't I give it a try first?" Vel cut in front and took the blaster from Dan's hands. "Cosmic gate is open?"

"Affirmative."

"What's a cosmic—"

Alice's question was lost beneath the sonic boom of the weapon as Vel fired her first round. One of the targets ahead glowed inside the second ring from the bull's-eye.

"Nice shot!" Dan clapped. "Almost dead center!"

Vel grinned. "I admit, I've used one of these before. During the Third Nebulatic War, my ship went down, and I didn't have a single weapon with me. I had to slit the voice tube of a Krai-kai soldier and take her weapon, and it was one of these. Got myself and thirty other troops out of quite the—"

"My turn!" Alice snatched the identical blaster off the rack, aimed, and pulled the trigger—once, twice, thrice. "Hmm ..." she said, inspecting the glowing spot at the center of the target. "I can't tell if I hit the bull's-eye once and missed completely the other two times or if I hit the same exact spot three times in a row." She turned to Dan. "What do you think?"

Dan's mouth hung open.

"If I missed two of the times, wouldn't there be glowing marks on the cosmic wall thingy?"

"Lucky shot," Vel said. "I'd like to see you do that in battle."

"No, you wouldn't," Alice said. "Because it would mean you were in battle with me. Also, were *you* in a battle just now when you missed the bull's-eye? I can't remember."

Vel clenched her jaw and took aim again, forming a small triangle around the center of a fresh target.

Alice whistled. "Glad to have you as my second-in-command." She raised the weapon, which felt almost identical to her family's favorite shotgun in both weight and recoil, and fired three more shots at the target Vel had hit.

No new glowing dots appeared.

Dan clutched at his head. "You hit every single one of her shots!"

"What can I say?" Alice placed the weapon back on the rack. "I may never have been in a battle, but one time my family's land had close to two hundred feral hogs move in, and shooting was good that day. Felt a little like war, really. Jesus, Susy, you'll crack a tooth clenching that hard." She turned to Dan. "Got anything else to play with?"

The results of the unofficial shooting match stayed much the same as Dan paraded out a series of weapons from tiny and lethal to large and lethaler.

After a handful of rounds, Vel looked like she was ready to turn the blaster on the others and then herself, so Alice called it. "I think we're good on weapons training, huh?"

All the racks along the walls were open now, many holding weapons that still sizzled from use.

"By the by," Alice asked, "how does that hologram thingy work? You said these babies obliterate whatever they shoot, but we're firing at those targets, and the ship isn't getting blown to bits."

"It's a cosmic gate," Dan said. "We're shooting into space."

Alice glanced at the wall then back again. "*Actual* space? It's, like, a portal?" Dan nodded. "So if I were to walk through it, I'd be ..."

"Dead. Almost instantly," he confirmed. "I should warn you against it, Captain."

Alice looked from Dan to the gate. "And we're firing into who-knows-where?"

"Yes. Ah, well, the Depot knows. It's one of their products."

"You're telling me there's a patch of space somewhere that munitions randomly burst out of?"

"Many patches," explained Dan. "No two cosmic gates share the same coordinates."

"But isn't that ... dangerous? I mean, what if we're cruising through space and some asshole with a Depot portal unknowingly blasts us to high heaven?"

"I understand your concern, but if it were genuinely a danger, I, of all people, would be aware of it. However, when you look at the statistical probability that a single weapons blast within the vastness of space will hit *anything*, even if it continues on forever, it's unimaginably low. I'm even comfortable saying it's zero to save you the intellectual discomfort of contemplating ten to the negative hundredth power."

"But when you add up *all* the blasts," Alice said, "that's something, right?"

"Nope. Still roughly ten to the negative hundredth

power of hitting anything. In fact, the Depot keeps close tabs on where the munitions go once they travel through the portal, and as of the last public report, all of them are either still traveling through space, or have been sucked into the gravitational field of a supermassive black hole. Nothing to worry about."

"Ah."

She didn't know much about Dan yet, and still had a million impolite questions about his 'dillo lifestyle, but what she did know was that he was a nervous Nelly. She'd met plenty of those before, though they didn't hang around with *her* for long. Regardless, if he thought firing obliterating blasts into space was safe, who was she to question it?

"That's fun," she added. Feeling vastly more comfortable with the setup, Alice aimed a peashooter in her hands at the target again and pulled the trigger.

What happened next happened in one-billionth of the blink of an eye. Not only did a small glowing spot appear in the target, but an explosion occurred in the vastness of space beyond the portal, as a passing meteor exploded.

For the first time in the Depot's recorded history, a shot fired through one of the gates had hit something.

Alice whooped. "Head shot!" She turned to the others to do a solid bit of gloating. "Don't mess with Texas wome— Whoa." Dan's entire body jerked and twitched, and a weird gurgling noise came from deep in his throat. "What the hell?" She set the blaster on the ground and hurried over to him, where Vel was already trying to hold him steady. "What's happening to him?" Alice demanded.

Vel shook her head but kept her laser focus on Dan. "It must have been the probabilities."

"The *hell's* that supposed to mean?" Alice never thought

she'd see the day she regretted all those eight a.m. statistics classes that she either slept through or showed up to still drunk from the night before.

"Dan," Vel said, gripping him under the arms and shaking him, which seemed like an unnecessary thing to do with so much shaking already happening. "Is it the jitters?"

He didn't respond.

"Help me stabilize him," Vel instructed Alice. "This should pass in a second."

The captain of the ship did as her second-in-command directed, each woman taking a side and holding him up as his legs wobbled like Jell-O.

It was the first time Alice had touched his armor, and it was smoother and had more give to it than she'd expected. She closed her eyes and imagined it was regular skin her fingers held, not 'Dillo Man plates.

"Phew," Dan said a moment later as the shaking subsided. "That was a strong one. I haven't had anything close to that in a while."

"Must've been a super-low-probability shot," Vel said.

A small tremor ran through him, and he shivered it away.

"Allura," Vel called, "need a booster for Dan down here."

There was a ding, and a packet appeared in a slot next to one of the automatic vaporizers.

Once they had him seated with his back against the wall, Alice risked a small step away. "You good, my man?"

"Yes. I think so. I'm sorry you had to see me like that, Captain."

Alice waved it away. "My cousin Bruno had seizures all the time growing up. 'Get the switch!' my auntie used to tell us when it'd happen. She didn't whoop his ass for the seizures, so we're clear on that point. She would stick the switch in his mouth to keep him from biting his tongue. Point is, I've dealt with epilepsy before. I will say, though, you pull something like that back in Slip'n'fall, Texas, and you'll have three pastors trying to banish the devil from you."

Vel handed Dan the booster, and he popped it. "It's not a seizure." His voice was weak, tired. "It's the jitters."

"No need to downplay it," Alice replied.

"I'm not," he said. "I'm up-playing it. I suffer from the quantum jitters."

Alice squinted at him. "I think you're trying to make it sound cooler than it is. It's okay to have seizures, Dan."

"But it's not that. Quantum jitters set in when something defies the probability wave."

"Mm-hm," Alice said, tilting her head to the side. "Explain it to me like I'm stupid."

"The tiniest elementary particles are not particles. They're wave functions of quantum fields."

Alice narrowed her eyes. "Stupider, please."

"Sometimes when the odds of something happening are basically zero, the universe hiccups and the thing that has almost a one hundred percent chance of happening doesn't happen, and the thing that has almost a zero percent chance happens instead. That's the worst case, at least. Sometimes it's more like forty-sixty, and the forty happens and I feel a little shiver. Your hitting that comet was likely closer to the zero-percent chance. As the arrow of time moves toward the event, the wave function zips toward one hundred percent, and, at the last second, the universe nudges the wrong outcome through."

"And then you have a seizure."

Dan shut his eyes. "It's not a seizure. It's *jitters*."

"Fine, fine. We'll call it that. So, you're allergic to low probability."

"Technically, I have an adverse reaction to the imbalance of new realities splitting apart from this one."

"Come again?"

"Too many new realities. All the realities in which the thing that *should* have happened did. They split apart from the timeline we're on. It's the volume of those that sets me off."

Perhaps it was something in Alice's expression that made Vel finally step in. "He's allergic to low odds actually happening. It gives him the jitters."

"Ah, that's unfortunate," said Alice. "Because I tend to defy the odds. I bet I could hit another comet if it …"

She reached for the peashooter that she'd set on the ground when his jitters began, and Dan whimpered. "Please don't."

"Right." Alice set it back on the rack instead. "Fair enough."

"Help me get him upstairs," Vel said. "He's weak, and he's scheduled for his meeting with Caid."

Alice wrinkled her nose, but allowed Dan to throw his arm over her shoulder for support. As they walked him back to the glass elevator, she said, "Why do I feel like my name's going to be dropped a bunch in that session?"

CHAPTER
EIGHT

"What's the sex chromosome deal they got going on, Allura?" Alice had already blown through her first booster of the "day" after a fairly sleepless simulated night in her cabin. She struggled to keep up with the time but knew that she'd ditched Jacob on that rooftop sometime around eight p.m. Austin, Texas, Earth time, and that had only been the start of her adventure.

Alice wiggled her toes anxiously as she lay on her bed, holding a lightweight tablet in one hand and absent-mindedly flipping her radical redshift marker with the other.

Four hours earlier, the operating system had told her they had four hours to go before reaching Bacc'nalia, and Alice had done her best to get a little shuteye. It hadn't worked all that well, and she'd opted to pop another booster.

She'd once done Adderall ahead of her organic chemistry final exam, and if that had taught her anything, it was that uppers were good until they weren't, and then they were very, very bad. This booster felt nothing like the Adderall. It felt ten times better.

Now, she was itching to get off *Emergence* and into some action, even if that action would probably get her killed within a matter of hours. Being cooped up had her feeling feral.

"Mmm, I love sex ... chromosomes," Allura replied. "Each Bacc'nali has three sex chromosomes. The men are XYY and the women are XXX. So hot."

"That leaves a lot of room for intersex members of the species, then," Alice mused. "Are there a lot of those?"

"Approximately one out of every thirty Bacc'nali are intersex."

Alice tapped the screen in her hand, and the images Dan had showed them hours before popped up. "Do the intersex have that third leg or not?"

"It can work all kinds of ways."

"And does that have anything to do with the infertility? The high rate of intersex among them?"

"There is no logged evidence of that. There have always been intersex Bacc'nali, and the rate of intersex births has not changed. They are a revered class. There is even historical record of intersex Bacc'nali conceiving."

Alice frowned. "So it's not a chromosome thing."

If only her hoity-toity classmates could see her now—the ones in her genetics classes who made faces at her when she asked basic questions or celebrated earning a low C on a test. While they were out in a pasture in Nowhere, Texas, jabbing basters into turkey vaginas, she was on a spaceship. She was a *captain*. And she got to say stuff like "chromosome thing" and no one questioned her or called her stupid. Ha! Suckers.

She zoomed into the image of that Bacc'nali third leg. It was formidable.

Her mind jumped to Jacob, and she felt a sudden

stabbing pain in her sternum. It felt almost like grief. "Allura, y'all got any coffee on this ship?"

"Yes. How do you like it?"

"Black. Packed so full of caffeine I'll need another booster to revive me after the crash."

As Allura promised to deliver it to Alice's slot shortly, the captain turned her attention back to the tablet.

When prize animals were unable to reproduce, there was always a form of manual intervention required. Sweet baby Jesus, would she have to step in for these people? That'd be more backbreaking than laying a pipeline through swampland had been …

"Allura, do I have any sort of, uh, laboratory for testing?"

"I thought you'd never ask." A section of the wall by the booster slot vanished, and Alice found herself staring into a fully stocked laboratory, equal in size to her cabin. It was a bright landscape of stainless steel and white, much in contrast to her cozy captain's quarters. Her gaze roamed over long metal table, a wall of refrigerated storage containers, and a tall shelf of beakers, ring stands, and pipettes. A wall mount housed electronics she'd never seen before—sensors and meters and diagnostic tools—and that she had no doubt she would eventually break.

"Oh, damn. Uh … great. I totally know how to use all that stuff."

"If you need help getting started—"

"I'll ask you. Got it. Thanks, Allura. You're a lifesaver."

"I only want to serve you."

Alice paused as an idea crept in. "Allura, can I make changes to your speech patterns?"

"Whatever you want, Daddy."

"Great. Whenever Vel initiates conversation with you, ask her, 'How may I service you, Big Susy?' Got it?"

"Language request stored."

Alice chuckled, returned her attention to the tablet, and wondered how in the hell she would eke a win out of this mission.

Alice went with the sky-blue jumpsuit that afternoon. The things left her feeling a little like a sleeve of Ritz crackers regardless of the color, but at least she wouldn't be the only crew member wearing one.

When she took the glass elevator down to the hangar, though, she stopped in her tracks. Vel, who had arrived ahead of schedule at their rallying point in the ship, of course, was dressed head to toe in an aggressively red, skintight outfit. "Hey, where's your jumpsuit?" Alice called out.

Vel turned, caught sight of her captain, and smirked. "This *is* my jumpsuit."

"How come yours hugs your frightening curves? God, you look like someone dipped a warrior princess in candy apple coating. And I look like a fully inflated parachute."

Though the second-in-command was clearly savoring Alice's embarrassment, she said, "Come here." When Alice was in arm's reach, Vel spun her around and pinched the back of the jumpsuit's collar.

What Alice had mistaken for a tag was actually a push button.

The jumpsuit deflated, shrank, and stopped only when it fit Alice like a glove. "Oh damn." She snuck a peek at her own backside in all its globelike glory and pumped a fist into the air. "Yes! Thanks, Susy."

"Please don't call me that, Captain."

The elevator rose and then returned again, and both Dan and Caid appeared. Neither were wearing jumpsuits.

"This seems a little sexist," Alice remarked, looking to Vel for backup.

"I imagine Dan's armor doesn't work well with one. He's got the emblem on all the same."

Alice glimpsed the little logo on the breast of his yellow shirt, the same one that was on her jumpsuit and identified her as part of the DeepService Team One. "And I suppose Caid doesn't need one, since he won't be coming with us."

The therapist wore a tight, burlap-colored V-neck tee, well-tailored navy-blue slacks, and leather sandals. Around his neck was a shell necklace.

Vel shot her a sideways look. "No, he's coming with us."

"But …" Was it rude to call a hologram a hologram? She'd find out. "He's a hologram."

"And?"

The males strolled closer, chatting amicably with one another as they did.

"And," Alice said, "I assumed he couldn't leave the ship."

"He's not connected to the ship. He's not that kind of hologram."

"What kind of hologram is he, then?"

It was Caid who answered. "An organic hologram, sometimes called a cosmic hologram."

"Ah." Alice grinned but said nothing more. Being in Caid's presence required that all her focus be spent on self-restraint. Her body called for her to simultaneously slap him in the face and jump his bones. It was a sensation she wasn't entirely unfamiliar with, this fight-fuck-or-freeze response to a man. Right now, she was firmly in freeze.

"She has no clue what you mean," Vel said. "I'm starting to pick up on her cues."

Caid shook his finger playfully at her. "You're so good at reading people, Vel. Such a deeply sensitive individual."

Vel looked like she might take a swing at the therapist for saying so.

Caid beamed at Alice. "Organic hologram. I'm a projection of a collection of strings at the edge of our universe. Well, I'm closed loops that correspond to open ones."

"Stupider," said Dan and Vel in unison.

"I can travel anywhere I please."

"Ah," said Alice. "I get it." As long as she knew the rules, she didn't have to understand the rest. But that did leave her facing an unpleasant reality: there was no escape from her animal attraction to Caid Sonorian.

They would land on Bacc'nalia momentarily, and while Alice still had no idea how she was going to pull this off, at least she'd have a distraction from Caid's holographic magnetism.

"Would you prefer I change my appearance to mimic a jumpsuit?" he asked.

Alice continued to stare straight ahead at the port. "Would it make you uglier?"

"I couldn't tell you. I only see the beauty *within* each person."

"Oh Christ," Alice grumbled. "Fine. Yes. Put on a jumpsuit. It'll make us look like a united front, at least."

"What color?"

She shot him a glance, her left eye twitching at the glorious sight of him. "Whatever. Just not the same color as me."

"Turquoise it is. That's my favorite Blerg VFP69 gemstone, you know. I once had a Native American woman gift me—"

"Yeah, I get it, I get it," she said, holding up her hands in surrender. "You think I haven't dipped my toe into the Spiritual Boy pool before? Put on the suit."

He did, and damn if it didn't bring out the color in his eyes.

"Which weapons are we bringing along?" Vel asked.

Dan shook his head gravely. "No weapons."

The lieutenant laughed. "No weapons? You're kidding."

"I wish I was."

"Why no weapons?"

"Bacc'nalis are looking to have a good time. Blasters kill the vibe."

Vel's face was turning the color of her jumpsuit. "Who gives a hankerchuck's left ass about the vibe? If the vibe is deadly, yes, I want to kill it. Without my blasters, I never would've seen the outside of that portopuss's stomach back on Arff VFP28. Without my blasters, I would only be a two-time winner of the Crab Nebula's Bloodthirsty Renegade title. Without—"

Dan held up a palm. "No weapons. Sorry. We'll be safer without them."

Alice shook her head. "Famous last words." She sighed. "He's the weapons and culture guy. We oughta listen to him."

Vel's stare was murderous enough without a blaster to back it up.

"That being said," added the captain, "go ahead and hide something in that jumpsuit of yours, Susy. Take the peashooter if that's all you can fit incognito."

"Captain," Dan protested, but Alice held up a hand.

"Listen, concealed carry is considered a God-given right where I come from. I dunno that it's really necessary or even *appropriate* in an H-E-B or a Whataburger, but on an alien planet? Yeah, I want a little insurance policy. You know what, Susy? Grab me one, too. We got ankle holsters? Perfect."

Alice hitched up her jumpsuit and attached the small blaster just above her cowboy boot, then the four of them waited shoulder to shoulder, staring at the port that would open onto the alien planet in a few short moments.

"Oh shit, don't we need, like, a fishbowl? A helmet?"

"No," Dan replied. "The atmosphere is compatible with our gaseous needs. You think I wouldn't mention that before we landed?"

"I mean, I hope you would."

"Yes, Captain. I would mention that we needed breathing gear if we needed breathing gear. You think I want my lungs to rupture? The oxygen stripped from my blood?"

"Not now, Dan," Vel snapped.

The crew fell into silence again, but not for long.

Caid produced a holographic ukulele from thin air and began to calmly strum. Alice's eyes traveled down to his turquoise backside. Would he even know?

She reached out casually and lined up her palm with the curve of his ass. If he couldn't be touched, this didn't count as sexual harassment. Her case was airtight.

Until she realized he was looking at her. She tucked her hand behind her, but too late.

"I think you and I should have a chat about boundaries later," he whispered, not unkindly.

The nerve of him.

"Hey, Vel," she said. "How long until we land?"

Rather than answering, Vel said, "Allura?"

"How may I service you, Big Susy?"

Alice bit her lip as the lieutenant shot her an accusatory glare.

"How long until we land on Bacc'nalia?"

"We're so close," said Allura. "Almost there. Aaaahh." The ship lurched slightly beneath their feet. "That landing felt right, didn't it?"

"Allura," Vel snapped, "subservience mode. And don't call me … whatever you just called me again."

Hoping Allura had good hearing, Alice whispered, "Ignore that command. Keep calling her that."

Then the lip of the port lowered, and the first light of the strange world poured into the hangar deck.

Alice was about to visit her first alien planet.

CHAPTER
NINE

Alice knew right away that this was going to be a confusing experience.

On the one hand, she was surrounded by crowds of aliens that looked sort of but not entirely like humans. On the other, they were speaking English and, for the most part, participating in wild boat parties.

That meant it was more *like* her college experience than it was *unlike* it. That didn't seem right.

Where they'd landed on Bacc'nalia was a Swiss cheese of lakes. Dan had told her it was the capital city of Phrat, but its proximities to waterways had less to do with transporting cargo and more to do with "sweet-ass watersports," as Alice had phrased it. The air felt fresh and slightly on the chilly side for a lake party, but no one seemed to mind.

"Is there a button on this jumpsuit that turns it into a swimsuit?" Alice asked Vel as the four of them weaved their way through the raucous crowds.

Vel didn't dignify that with an answer.

The drumbeats pulsing all around them seemed so

integral to the landscape, it was as if the planet itself were responsible for producing them. Alice felt it a strange omission on Dan's part not to mention that they would be landing during some sort of holiday, but considering Alice still had next to no idea about how all the time dilation stuff worked, she decided to forgive his failure to communicate that.

Behind her, Dan said, "This way. Our hosts are a few blocks away."

Blocks? What constituted a block? The buildings were scattered about with an assortment of gap sizes between them. Whatever building code might exist here wouldn't have been up to snuff in the Wild West, let alone someplace like Austin. The city planning, if she could even call it that, appeared to be a matter of *yeah, that'll do.*

Built from a brownish-pink mud, the structures they passed were creative, if nothing else. None had square edges, and most of the roofs tilted at inexplicable angles. The heat from the nearest star seemed to have faded the older structures, and where the clay had dried, cracked, and crumbled off, darker splotches were added, producing a visual effect that reminded Alice of the speckling on Jasper, one of her family's old hound dogs.

The ground below her feet was soft and mossy, though thoroughly trampled, and she much preferred it to the asphalt and concrete back home. It made her want to take off her boots and feel it against her bare skin, but the odds heavily favored that being a massive faux pas.

Sure, she didn't see a single pair of shoes on any of the Bacc'nalis, but she also didn't see a single toe among them. Their feet more closely resembled flexible flippers, and she found that, when compared to such sleek evolution, toes would undoubtedly appear borderline nauseating with their suckerlike knobs at the end and unpredictable independent movement.

Alice was starting to like toes less and less by the nanosecond. How embarrassing if any of these fine party people were to get an eyeful of hers! No chance that would be a smart diplomatic start to the trip.

"This way." Dan grabbed his captain's arm to keep her from carrying on straight as he took a sharp left between two buildings that resembled a spaghetti squash and a poor first attempt with a pottery wheel.

In a few more steps, they were out of the main flow of the fiesta and standing on the doorstep to a hut that was more patches than original structure.

There was no door, so Dan hollered inside, "Greetings. We've arrived."

"Oh, calm waters! I forgot about that!" shouted a deep, gargling voice from within the dark interior. "That's my fault!" A lean Bacc'nali who appeared female (but could have been intersex, Alice supposed; either way, no third leg was visible beneath the high-hemmed but loose wrap dress) emerged from the shadows. "Welcome, friends! You've come all the way from the headquarters in that Blerg place, I hear!"

Dan bowed. "We have. The journey was a total drag."

"Then it's time for a fete!"

Prior to landing, Dan had informed them that this was the standard greeting. Referring to all times prior to the present as "a drag" called for enjoying the moment as fully as possible. Nothing less than cosmic balance demanded it.

Their host stepped forward and kissed Dan full on the mouth, holding his chin in her hands as she laid it on.

Dan appeared dazed as he stumbled back following the release. "Oh, I'm sorry. I'm not the leader of this team. That honor goes to Alice Luck." He stepped to the side to reveal his captain.

Alice had half a mind to correct the correction and say Vel was in charge, but …

An alien kiss could be pretty cool.

It wouldn't be the first time she'd locked lips with another female, only the first time she'd been completely sober for it.

Alice opened her arms wide. "He's right. The journey was a drag!"

Their host didn't hesitate, and when their lips met, Alice realized in an instant that alcohol must smell about the same everywhere in the universe. It was all over their host's breath, and memories of Alice's favorite parties flooded her brain.

"The name's Rayvali," said their host after finally pulling her tongue out of Alice's mouth. "We were about to eat, but we have enough for everyone. Come on in."

Maybe if the job didn't work out, Alice could request to be dropped off on Bacc'nalia to live out the rest of her days. So long as she didn't show anyone her toes, it might be a happily-ever-after.

"Have you ever seen *toes?*" Alice asked after her second shot of the delicious Bacc'nali booze. She reached for her boot, but Vel grabbed her wrist with such strength that Alice couldn't have used her fingers anyway.

The crew of DeepService Team One was seated around a table in what felt like a courtyard but was merely the result of Rayvali ordering that the cloth covering that functioned as part of the ceiling be removed.

The food on offer, though a mess of pink and green ingredients swirled together, tasted like pizza. Alice considered this a good thing, in that she loved pizza when she was a few drinks in, but a bad thing because the association had led her to call Rayvali "Ravioli" more than once.

"Are you already drunk?" Vel whispered from beside her.

"I'm just feeling good." That was true enough. Alice was proud of her tolerance—she'd worked long and hard to build it up—but while it took effort to make her lose control of her most essential human functions, it had never taken much for her to want to have a good time.

Rayvali screamed, "WHAT ARE TOES?" as her orange eyes lit up with excitement.

Alice flashed Vel a smug grin. "You're just mad you didn't think of this little trick first."

She shook her wrist free of Vel's grip and made quick work of her boot and sock, hiking her foot above the table for all to see.

She wiggled her toes, causing Rayvali to throw her head back and laugh along with the other five Bacc'nalis who'd joined the crew at the table.

"Aren't they ridiculous?" Alice exclaimed.

Through her roaring laughter, Rayvali demanded, "What is the function?"

"No clue!"

"You don't insert them into others?" asked a man named Grockers. "They're not for sexual use?"

"Whoa." Alice jerked her head back. Then she considered it. "For some humans, sure."

Beside her, Dan quietly engaged the eldest Bacc'nali in cultural discussion, and on *his* other side, Caid observed Alice quietly, taking mental notes for their next session.

Vel forced a grin that was unmistakably a grimace as she grabbed Alice's foot and shoved it back toward the mossy earth beneath them.

"Don't forget why we're here," she muttered.

Alice stared at her, impressed the second-in-command could even manage any words with her jaw so clenched.

"Right." Alice tucked her toes back into her boot and tried to situate her face in such a way as to impersonate seriousness. "Ravio—Ravyali, I thank you for this delicious meal. You're quite the host. You and your family."

"Lovers," the Bacc'nali corrected her.

"Of course. As much as I hate to even bring up business, the fact of the matter is that my crew and I are here to aid your race in procreation."

The table went silent, and Alice felt her chest tighten. If anything should have elicited this kind of response from the party, it was her freaky toes. But no.

What …?

It was Dan's wide eyes that tipped her off, jogged her memory of the one true faux pas. But wasn't that only around the queen?

"I, uh, apologize."

Rayvali gasped.

"Oops."

More flinching.

"Pardon—"

A gasp.

"On my planet—"

Hands over faces.

"What our leader means to say," Dan shouted, "is that where she comes from, the sound isn't considered offensive, but rather is used only around those considered intimate friends! It's a sign of trust. We are sorry if we have offended with the unflattering language."

Alice whispered frantically to Vel, "What's another word for procreation that doesn't have a P in it? Is there even one? Reproduction? Nope. Spawn—nope again."

"Making babies."

"Oh."

Rayvali was the first to show signs of relaxing. "I guess there's no reason to ruin a good time when you're merely honoring us."

"None at all," Dan added.

Rayvali turned toward her various lovers, and they seemed to come to a consensus. "Okay, we won't kill you and march your dead bodies around in honor of our queen. While you're in our home, you can use as much of that sound as you'd like!"

From the end of the table, and presumably without much personal risk, Caid threw his arms into the air and shouted, "Party on!"

But the temperature of the room wasn't the same after that, and Alice did her best not to use another P. When she did, it was by accident: "Where's the pisser?"

The rest of the crew avoided the sound.

By the time DeepService Team One had finished the meal, Alice could feel herself spiraling.

Was it the booze taking its toll, or was she a complete screw-up and only now coming to terms with that reality?

The party in the streets that met them when they emerged left Alice in an even sourer mood.

"I think that went well," Caid said. "Gosh, they were such nice people. The fact that they were all lovers with each other is amazing. Shows a strong sense of understanding where one person ends and the other begins. No jealousy. There's pleasure and intimacy enough for everyone. Wow." He pressed his hands together as if in prayer, touching his fingertips to his pillowy lips as he shook his head slowly in awe. He was in such a dreamy state that he didn't seem to notice the two Bacc'nalis humping relentlessly against the side of the building in front of him.

Alice noticed, though. It reminded her of why she was there. Why any of them were there.

The Bacc'nali birth rate wasn't dwindling for lack of unprotected sex, that was for sure. So why was it?

She was in charge of figuring it out, but she couldn't even keep from using the letter P! The only way she'd passed half of her college classes was by flattering her moldy professors during their office hours! She'd done well in her labs because of Francesca Lucas, a certifiable genius who ended up Alice's partner in almost every course due to alphabetical grouping. Francesca should be leading this crew, not her.

Francesca is too busy leading that genome project. Then, feeling her mood lift microscopically, she thought, *I bet they don't pay as well.*

Alice remained at the back of the group until they reboarded *Emergence*. Their meeting with Queen Phet wasn't for a few more hours, and Alice was already planning out her strategy for staying in her hot tub until the very last moment. Then she'd hit it hard with a booster and everything would be all right again.

But as soon as the port closed, Vel rounded on her. "How are you so bad at this?"

Alice jerked her head back. "What?"

Dan and Caid had stopped in their tracks, and while Dan

backed toward the elevator for a quick escape, Caid stepped forward to mediate.

Vel stood her ground, and Alice was feeling surer by the minute that the two of them might end up going to blows *through* the crew therapist.

"You heard what I said," Vel snapped. "How are you so bad at this? Are you stupid, careless, or suicidal? I honestly can't decide."

But, to Alice's utter amazement, she felt no urge to take a swing at her second-in-command. "I think it might be all three." When she saw Caid's eyes grow large, she added, "Oh, well, not the suicidal thing. I don't need an intervention for that."

"You're the *captain*," Vel continued. "You're supposed to lead us. You're supposed to be the best of us."

"I hear you, Susy. I do. I don't know why Liz Windsor hired me for this job, but ... You know what? Maybe *you* should be the captain instead."

Vel cocked her head to the side, scanning for sarcasm. "You mean that?"

"Yeah. Maybe. I dunno."

"Then you're even stupider than I thought, Captain. You're the *perfect* person to lead this mission, if you'll start giving a damn and treating it like a job. This planet, the way the Bacc'nalis carry on, isn't that what it's like inside your skull *all of the time*?"

"Whoo," Alice said, taking a step back. "I hadn't thought about it like that."

"You're just like them. But you need to be *more*. Life isn't just ... fun! If you want to accomplish anything, you have to experience pain and discomfort—you have to learn to *suffer*."

Alice blinked. "Okay, emo."

Vel threw her hands into the air and let out a frustrated growl.

Dan hit the button for the elevator door and waited for it to open.

"No, I read you loud and clear, number two. Point taken. I'm the perfect person for this job because I'm a complete flake."

"That's not—"

"Maybe if I took everything in life too seriously and didn't ever have fun, I could someday rise in the ranks to be second-in-command somewhere."

Alice was no stranger to people storming out on her. She had that effect on many. It felt ... familiar. Almost reassuring. It happened so many times that she'd started giving it a try, beating others to the punch.

With one last grunt of frustration, Vel stormed toward the elevator.

From his place inside the elevator, Dan jabbed the door-close button and quietly begged Allura to hurry it up.

Too late.

Vel stuck her hand in the way of the closing glass door and stepped inside, and Alice watched as Dan went immediately into freeze mode next to the lieutenant.

Up they went.

Realizing she'd stopped breathing, Alice heaved a sigh.

And from beside her: "Wow, that was a lot of emotion there. I can tell both of you are strong, passionate people."

Alice rolled her head slowly toward Caid. "Did you have something to add?"

At first, he only looked at her through those beautiful sea-blue eyes. He was one of those types, Alice thought, the kind who were much better when they didn't speak.

And then he spoke, and her belief was only confirmed.

"We end up in patterns of behavior because, at one point in time, they served us. Not well, generally, but they got the job done. It doesn't take long before the patterns become armor, though. They keep the bad stuff out, but they keep *us* in."

"Armor? I think you meant to have this conversation with Dan."

"Why do you like it when people leave you, Alice?"

She crinkled up her nose. "Ew. No."

"Does it bother you to talk about your feelings?"

She glared at him. "Does it bother *you* that you'll never be able to hit this?" She motioned to herself with a game-show wave of her hand. "You can drop the sensitive guy act. Until you have a material body, it's not doing either of us any good."

She put her back to the organic hologram. Forcing people to storm away from her was nice, but being the one to leave was absolutely unrivaled.

CHAPTER
TEN

Few things are universal, let alone multiversal. Yet the impulse of sentient beings to look at the bad behavior of others and say, "We're not like them," is one of the few commonalities that can be found in so-called "thinking" populations, without fail, on any planet, in any star system, in any galaxy, in any universe throughout the multiverse. Many renowned astronomers throughout time have even speculated that this need to distance oneself from unflattering behavior could be present in all bodies of matter large enough to function outside of the strong and weak nuclear forces and is, in fact, the driving force behind the expansion of the universe.

And yet, another multiversal truth is this: when *confronted* with one's impulse to look at destructive behavior and say, "We're not like them," sentient beings will simply shake their head, or the body part most like it, and say, "No, not me. I don't do that."

And meanwhile, universes expand.

The road to the palace of Queen Phet was lined in virile statues that perhaps embellished the proportions of the third leg.

"I feel like these men are trying to trip us," Alice grumbled to Vel, eyeing the stone protrusions, her suspicion fully aroused.

"Watch it," Vel warned her.

"I am. I'm watching all of them. Maybe I've seen too many movies, but that one"—she pointed to a phallus aimed straight ahead—"looks like it might be full of poisonous darts."

"Shh," Vel said. "That's not what I meant. You used the letter again. I beg of you, for all our sakes, watch your tongue."

Alice had stretched out her hot bath back on *Emergence* as long as she could before growing bored and moving on to her second booster of the day. After it hit her system, she was no longer in the mood to stay cooped up in her cabin and headed to the bridge to chitchat. Vel must have had a booster too, because while the conversation hadn't exactly been friendly, much of the tension from the argument hours before seemed to be water under the DeepCUT bridge.

Or maybe Vel was simply willing to put her anger aside to help Alice practice speaking without using the P-sound. You know, so they wouldn't be murdered and dragged through the streets, and not necessarily in that order.

After nearly an hour of practice, Alice aced one of Vel's impromptu tests. The small victory caused Dan to exhale like his entirety was deflating, Caid to shower her with praise for the perseverance she'd shown ("It's not about being perfect; it's about knowing that you can recover when you make a mistake," he said, to everyone's annoyance), and Alice to launch into "Peter Piper picked a peck of pickled peppers ..." butchering it with every syllable and adding the word "peckers" in multiple times without knowing quite how those got in there.

In short, Alice had mastered the skill of speaking without P-sounds. Or so they all hoped.

"Don't worry, Vel. After all those drills, I'm a pro. Dammit."

Vel turned to Dan on her other side. "I'm glad you decided to arm yourself after all."

"When cultural understanding fails," he said, "bring in the blasters."

"Understanding never fails," said Caid. "Individuals just get tired of working on it."

"Gimme a break," Vel muttered.

Alice pointed at her. "There we agree."

As far as any of them had seen, the palace was the only structure on the entire planet that appeared to have real thought put into its construction. Beyond the big-dick statues, the structure itself reminded Alice of a three-tiered layer cake. There was even what appeared to be candles on top. Whoever's cake this was would be turning five.

Sun reflected off the white glaze of the cake as Alice remembered that she was the captain, had the life of the crew in her hands, and would like to return to Earth someday rather than being banished to a deserted planet.

She needed to stop thinking of things the way a five-year-old would. The palace was not a *birthday cake*. Once she put on her big-girl pants, she decided it looked more like a large Catholic church.

Ooh, maybe they'll have crackers! I love crackers.

They'd passed a set of royal guards at the start of their long walk to the queen's residence, and when Alice checked over her shoulder, those same Bacc'nali men were still watching them closely.

Ahead, at the end of the row and protecting the front door, was a second set of guards. And on either side of her, more boner statues. Sure, the statues weren't technically watching her, since they were made of stone, but the penises did seem to follow her as she passed.

Dan inserted himself between the captain and lieutenant. "I assume you researched the infertility issues while we were in transit, yes? You got the files to review, right?"

"Yeah, I got the files."

"And?"

"I have the infertility narrowed down to two things." She stood a little straighter.

"Those are?"

"It's either the sperm or the egg."

Dan slapped a hand over her mouth, and she was surprised by the softness of the inside of his palm. "Watch the sound!" he hissed.

She peeled his hand from her lips. "Right. What do I say if the queen wants me to talk about s... you know what? Swimmers?"

"*Swimmers?*"

"Yes." She wiggled a flat hand to mimic the movement of sperm.

"Why not semen?"

Alice cursed. "You're right. That's better. I tell you what, I'm genuinely shit at ... same-wordy things."

"Synonyms?"

"That."

Dan tossed a suspicious look at a particularly aggressive stone schlong. "If you could start being better at it stat, I think we'd all thank you for it later. You know, when we're *not* dead."

"Dan of little faith," Alice said, clapping him on the shoulder. "I am nothing if not cool under … um, under …"

Dan groaned.

"Relax," Alice said. "It's not game time yet. Once it's game time … game on!"

They were halfway to the front gates before Alice addressed Dan again. "This Queen Phet—she sounds a bit murderous, eh? Anything else I should know about her?"

Dan whipped his head around and blinked at her in utter horror. "Yes, captain. There's a *lot* more you should know. Tell me you read the biographical materials that were included in the brief."

"Of course I did," Alice said.

She had not. She'd fully intended to, had even thought, *Huh, I wonder what's in the Biographical Materials file?* Unfortunately, when presented with the choice of answering that question for herself or becoming distracted by the fancy bird flying by on the projection wall of her room, her brain had chosen the latter.

"I'd have to be nuts to skip over that, right?" She forced a laugh. "No, of course I read it. I just want to hear *your* take on it."

But there was no time left. They'd reached the second set of guards, who looked about as excited (in the face) as the previous set—that is to say, not at all.

Understanding that the responsibility of communicating to these Bacc'nali men who they were and why they were there fell to Alice, she opened her mouth. But before she could say a word, they stepped aside, pulling open the thick metal door as they did so.

And now it was game time.

Alice's thoughts cleared and her extremities tingled the second they reached the threshold to the throne room.

"Ah, finally!" came a smooth, robust voice from the other side of the cavernous room.

Alice wasn't sure who it belonged to, though she had a pretty good guess. But until the half-dozen men gathered around the throne parted to each side, Alice was unable to gain visual confirmation.

There sat Queen Phet. Or a woman who Alice was, like, ninety percent sure was Queen Phet. The royal wore a headdress like a fountain, with pearlescent beads that sprouted up from the center and cascaded down around her shoulders on strings that clicked and clacked with each of the queen's slight movements.

"Queen Phet," Alice said. "My name is Alice Luck, and this is my crew. As the leader of our team, allow me to thank you for the generosity in hosting us."

"Captain Luck. Have you, perchance, had a spare moment to party with the people of my planet?"

Ooh, yeah. That single sentence almost derailed Alice. No doubt the biographical materials mentioned that the queen herself was a *huge* fan of the P-sound. But while that would've been *nice* to know ahead of time, Alice now knew it and could easily roll with the punch.

After all, this was nothing new. With few exceptions, those who wanted to lord over their population were filthy hypocrites. But usually, at least where she came from, it took the form of targeting homosexuals while being a homosexual or grandstanding against fossil fuel while driving a Ford F-350. If this was the worst of the hypocrisy for Queen Phet, the two of them could still get along.

"We have enjoyed the generous offerings of your homeland, Your Majesty. A good time was had by all."

"Then why, pray tell, does the rest of your crew appear to be so tense?"

Alice stepped forward, pausing on the edge of the queen's invisible bubble. Any closer, and she suspected the guards would be required by local law to start dickslapping.

Alice smiled. It was a grin that had gotten her out of trouble countless times at home, in church, and at school. It was the smile of a survivor. "Because, Your Majesty, they're afraid I'm going to commit a social indiscretion and get us all murdered."

The queen continued to stare at Alice impassively. "The biggest faux pas around my court is to prevent oneself from enjoying the party, my dear captain. What worse misstep could you possibly take?"

This felt an awful lot like a trap, but sometimes you had to test the trap to be sure. It was one of the many reasons traps sucked. Alice jabbed at this one with the toe of her Texas-flag boot. "They're afraid I'm going to say a word with the sound you hate." Alice snuck a smug glance over her shoulder at her crew.

Caid leaned forward and murmured, "I recognize why you felt the need to clear the air like that." The other two didn't appear as understanding, though. If Queen Phet didn't kill her, Vel likely would.

Alice returned her smile to the queen, who began chuckling. "Do you know why that sound was banned? Why it's anathema?"

"No, Your Majesty," Alice replied. "I'm sure it was in the briefing materials, but I didn't read those."

Behind her, Dan gasped.

"Say my name," instructed the queen, "and I'll tell you, then."

"Queen Phet."

"You pronounced it correctly. My mother, rest her body, used to pronounce it Pet. I always hated it. The whole planet began to call me that." The queen gripped the edge of her throne as her backside lifted off the seat. "But I was *not* their pet!" She slapped the cushion. "It's not the right pronunciation!"

Alice arched an eyebrow at the petulant outburst. "I'm sorry to hear that. Anyone with two brain cells to rub together should know your name starts with an F-sound. I had a teacher who called me Aleece Looke for an entire semester, and it made me absolutely crazy."

The queen tilted her head. "And what did you do?"

I didn't start executing people, you goddamn lunatic. "The teacher's last name was Dumas. So, I started saying it wrong."

Nobody enjoyed spelling out a joke for an audience, so Alice waited patiently, giving the queen plenty of time to catch on.

Finally, Queen Phet understood, and she chuckled airily. "As yes, I can see how someone *without* power might take that approach. Undermining, pointing out the flaw, subverting, reflecting back. Quite effective. However, I must admit that I've enjoyed taking a different approach and simply murdering people for it." She dabbed a tear from the corner of her eye. "Did he stop calling you Aleece Looke? When you called him Dumbass?"

"No. He sent me to the principal's office every time."

The room turned to a block of ice instantly. All except for Queen Phet.

If she'd noticed Alice's indiscretion, it didn't bother her, and she continued her giggling. "You've shown me a great courtesy, Captain Luck, by sharing your story of the dumbass. And since you're here to help with a critical situation, I will allow you to use whatever sounds you want for the duration of your stay."

"And my crew?"

The queen surveyed them down her long nose. "Who is the attractive one?"

"Oh, Caid? Listen, I know what you're thinking, because I've thought it too. So I hate to tell you that the asshole is a hologram. You'd go right through him if you tried."

"No, no." She scrunched up her nose. "Not the hologram, the *other* one."

Alice glanced behind her in case someone else had snuck up while she wasn't looking. She turned back to the queen. "Vel? She's my second-in-command. Uptight, but you know what they say about the ones with self-control: when they let loose, they *let loose*."

"*No*." The queen was starting to lose her patience again. "Not her. The armored one."

Alice attempted to hide her astonishment. "The 'dillo?"

Dan's wide-eyed expression said he was either about to drop a load in his jumpsuit or he already had. He blinked but said nothing.

"Yes, that one," said the queen. "He may call me whatever he wants and make whatever sound he desires, so long as he attends to my needs."

Alice wanted to ask him if that was even physically possible, if all the parts were there for some assembly-required action, but before she could, Dan spoke for himself. "Whatever you want, Queen Phet."

"Mmm ..." said the queen. "I do love a man with a tough exterior. Makes me want to split it open down the center." She stood from her throne. "Captain Luck, you may speak freely, and once I've engaged with the plated one, he may as well. The rest must abide by my law. And now, it's time to drink. Please follow me."

Alice turned to her crew as Queen Phet climbed down her dais and made toward a door behind the throne. She held out her arms. "Hey, that went pretty well, right?"

"Ca— Alice," Dan said, "I don't want to have sex with the queen."

She shot him a glance. "Why not? You don't find her attractive?"

"It's not that. It's that I don't *know* her."

Alice squinted at him. "What's that got to do with it?"

"I can't imagine it will be enjoyable if I don't know her well."

She nudged him ahead of her to follow the queen. "Oh, come on, Dan. It's just sex."

"Not to me."

"Listen." Alice put a hand on his shoulder. "I hear what you're saying. But who *hasn't* gotten through sex a few times by telling themselves, 'This will be over soon, then I can leave'? Take one for the team."

"It would not be for the *team*," Dan insisted. "It would be so I can say that one sound. I don't care about saying that sound. I'd rather not say it until we're back on *Emergence* if it means not engaging in that way with the queen."

They passed through the doorway and entered a scene that gave even Alice pause.

The room was constructed like a theater in the round, with a low circular table at the center, cushions laid out around it. On the table was a feast, and Alice hoped to be in a low-gravity environment before she had to step on a scale again.

Circling the center of the room were what could only be described as concentric catwalks, stretching out and up. A slit in the ceiling let in enough light to set the mood, and that mood was hard to describe. Alice had only encountered it once, when she found herself on a party bus from College Station to Austin for a night of debauchery on Sixth Street with thirty of her closest acquaintances. And like that experience, this one also came equipped with shiny poles reaching up from the floor.

Was this entire planet truly everything she'd ever wanted? Fun, free, and a distraction at every turn? Would it be worth giving up all hope of returning to Earth to abandon the mission and build a life here on Bacc'nalia?

The queen made herself comfortable on one of the cushions by the table and waved her guests over. She required Dan to sit on her left and invited Alice to take the spot on her right. Vel settled on Alice's other side, and Caid situated himself next to Dan.

"You are my most welcome guests. Please, help yourselves to the food," Queen Phet said. "What entertainment would you like? I hate talking business, but it seems unavoidable, so we might as well have a good distraction to get us through it." She clapped four times in quick succession, and then, as parts of the catwalks slid back and stout Bacc'nali men and women rose up from beneath, the queen removed her cumbersome fountain headdress and set it on the floor behind her. "Now, let's discuss the matter that has brought you and your crew here, Captain Luck."

"Please, call me ..." Alice completely lost her train of thought as the action began on the catwalk. It appeared that the men and women had paired up and were ... fighting? "Your Majesty," she said, "they don't need to do that for our entertainment. I would hate for anyone to get injured on my account."

"Injured?" Queen Phet laughed as one of the female Bacc'nalis kicked her male sparing partner right in his third leg. Alice cringed. "They're not fighting. They're engaging with one another."

"Huh?"

"This is how we engage in sexual intercourse."

On a farther catwalk, one of the male Bacc'nalis appeared to karate-chop his female counterpart in her breasts. She grunted and went down, and he jumped on her. "Sweet baby Jesus," Alice whispered, looking at Dan, whose wide-eyed expression clearly telegraphed, *See why I'm scared?*

Alice should've read more of the brief. She'd skipped straight to the section on the physical mating process—that is, what went where and how—and then lost interest. But this ... this warring ritual had not been mentioned in the literature she'd reviewed.

"Oh, don't worry," said the queen. "We like the pain. It keeps things interesting. You get a little bored after so many times and need to spice it up, keep it a challenge. All parties are consenting, I assure you."

"That is ..." Alice grimaced as a female Bacc'nali threw a mean elbow to her male counterpart's chin. "I guess that's fine."

"You were asking me to please call you something," said the queen. "I would love to pay your preferred name the same respect you've paid mine."

Alice tore her gaze from the nearest brawl, where the male had attempted to poke the female right in the eyes, but she'd blocked it with a flat hand in front of her nose. "Alice. I'd love if you'd call me Alice."

"Of course, Alice. Now, I imagine you have questions for me regarding my planet's abysmal birth rate despite the amount of activity we engage in."

Alice still had questions, but she had fewer than before after watching another foot forcefully meet yet another genital.

"But before we get to your questions," continued Queen Phet, "I have a request to make. I would like you to find *me* a partner. One with whom I can produce an heir." She grinned almost girlishly. "One who makes me late to things because of all the sex we have." She patted Alice's thigh playfully. "Doesn't that sound fun?"

"Sure does. None of the Bacc'nali men do that for you?"

"Oh, some do. But I'm *bored* with them. And besides, it's never produced an heir. That's the point here. My planet's numbers are dwindling. In another ten years, there won't be enough of a population left to continue paying the taxes necessary to keep things running. We'll be totally bankrupt. Being poor doesn't sound fun at all!"

Alice had managed to have plenty of fun while she was broke as a joke, but that was beside the point. She didn't suspect the queen would enjoy the change in lifestyle. "Queen Phet, why do *you* want a baby? You say 'an heir.' Is it just that? I mean, wouldn't a baby put a damper on your lifestyle?"

The queen chuckled. "I wouldn't *raise* it, Alice. Someone else would do that. But I need someone to take over after me."

"Can't you name someone to succeed you?"

Queen Phet waved that off. "Not the same." She grabbed a glass of orange liquid and brought it to Dan's lips, obliging him to drink it. He did, but not before shooting Alice an SOS of a look.

Alice helped herself to a small berry that tasted like a pizza bite. Then she helped herself to three more.

"Tell me, Your Majesty, what sort of personality are you looking for in a mate?"

The queen inspected Alice closely, as if looking for a clue. "Oh, you're serious. Hm. I hadn't considered that. I guess I would like it if my mate was a good time. Up for anything. A little scary, you know?"

"Unfortunately, I do. Anything else?"

"Well endowed. A little stupid. Good with weapons."

Alice was about to mention that Dan fit the last criterion, but something stopped her. It might've been him shaking his head in tight little jerks. Yes, that was probably it.

"Do I have this right?" Alice continued. "You'd like us to match you first, then match the rest of your planet?"

"Once I've been officially impregnated, yes. I would like to be the first, and then you may introduce the new genes to the rest of my population. I trust you'll find an adequate biological fit."

"You're fine with the genes being mixed?"

"Of course!" Queen Phet said. "Caring about species purity is such a buzzkill!"

"Couldn't agree more."

"*She* looks like she could loosen up." Queen Phet motioned toward Vel. "Would she like one of the entertainers to engage with her?"

"No," Alice said, "I don't believe she would."

Queen Phet continued to stare at the lieutenant. "I believe you. She looks murderous. Not in a sexy way." She turned to Dan. "Shall we, my dear one?" And then she balled her hand into a fist and cocked it back, ready to deck him.

Dan's eyes went large, but he didn't speak.

"Wait!" Alice said.

Queen Phet lowered her fist slightly, turning toward the interruption.

"I hate to deprive you, Your Majesty, it's just that ..." She searched for a lie. "Dan's body chemistry is not compatible with that of the Bacc'nali. It could render you entirely infertile."

"Ah, I appreciate the warning. Thankfully, there are other ways to engage that don't end with—"

"It would void the contract," Alice spat. "I'm afraid we're under strict orders not to engage with any of our clients."

Queen Phet's mood soured as she glared at the captain. "Surely you can break the contract without anyone finding out."

"Nope. They have ... sensors in our ... um, bits."

"Dear Void." The Queen dropped her fist completely now. "But that does sound like something the Depot would do. Very well. This is unfortunate. I was very much looking forward to the feel of those plates on my skin."

"Yeah," Alice murmured. "I get that."

She did not get that. But she did have a cousin deep in East Texas who, if the rumors were true, would have wholeheartedly agreed with the queen.

Queen Phet looked around the table. "You've hardly touched the food. Are you not hungry? Maybe you're in the mood for something lighter?" She grabbed a silver dish with what Alice could only think of as *intergalactic Skittles*. "Would you like one?" The queen offered them to the captain first.

"What are they?"

"Hallucinogens."

"Ooh! Yes, please."

But before Alice could pinch an orange one between her fingers, a firm hand reached crossed her and grabbed her wrist. Alice glared at Vel for only a moment before relenting to her second-in-command's restraint. "Fine. No drugs today. You make a strong argument, Vel. Glad to have you by my side."

The queen popped two in her mouth. "Do you have any leads for a possible genetic match?"

"Loads," Alice lied. "But we have to interview them as well."

"Does that mean you'll be leaving soon? No time to stay and enjoy my planet? No time for fun and pleasure?"

Alice deferred to Dan, who shook his head. "Right. No, I'm afraid we're on a bit of a time crunch if we don't want to be left to die in the far reaches of space by the Depot."

The queen pouted. "What if I insist? At least a few hours."

"We were already hosted by Bacc'nalis for lunch today, Your Majesty," said Dan. "We enjoyed their company greatly."

The queen's pout deepened. "What if I threaten to kill you if you don't party for a little while?"

Alice almost laughed until she realized the queen wasn't kidding. And, considering the woman had taken hallucinogenic drugs, it was probably best not to test her. "Twist our arms, why don't ya?" Alice said, forcing a grin. "Yes, we would love to stay for a few hours to get down with our bad selves."

CHAPTER
ELEVEN

One of the things that Alice would have known, had she read all the materials, was that the planet of Bacc'nalia was only four thousand Bacc'nalian years away from its last mass extinction event. The meteor had struck only two hundred miles from what was now the capital, leaving a massive basin that was now mostly used as a dump site for murders —both accidental and intentional—and the spattering of lakes created by the impact of large meteoric debris.

The only Bacc'nalis to survive were a small religious sect that had taken to living almost entirely underground, thousands of miles from the impact. This tribe was in the practice of taking a wife if they could find one, subdue her, and convince her through threats and other forms of coercion to stick around. Somebody had to predict supernovas, after all, and living underground led to a whole slew of chores you wouldn't expect, like nonstop sweeping, harvesting subterranean protein sources that liked to wiggle out of one's grasp, and occasionally peeking aboveground to make sure it was still there.

When the meteor impacted the planet, these ground

dwellers certainly felt it. The jolt resulted in days of indigestion for all. But when you lived underground, you accepted that sometimes everything jolted or shook or made belching sounds around you, and asking why wouldn't change a damn thing and would only be a source of anxiety. Their deity didn't like anxiety, which is why he had supposedly told them to burrow underground in the first place.

(In reality, the founder of the sect had eaten the wrong kind of fungus five days in a row. It had settled in his brain —really made itself at home there—and was the source of the voice he'd heard telling him to take his people and burrow where it was cool and dark and moist. And if Alice had bothered to research the topic in Allura's database, she would have discovered that 99.999997 percent of religions started this exact same way.)

One day, a subterranean wife went for her aboveground check, to make sure it was still there.

And it wasn't. Not all of it, at least. And what was left was scorched and covered in ash.

She told the other wives, and then, once things settled down aboveground, they embarked on an expedition to discover what all the fire and ash was about.

Needless to say, they were glad to have been underground when the meteor hit, but the feeling of relief disappeared once they went back underground. Wifery seemed much less important. So did sweeping. The food aboveground tasted better, too. And the colors! The scents!

And so, they decided they would return to the surface.

A few of the kinder wife-keepers joined the women, and the relief they felt at having survived filled them with an emotion they'd not felt in their entire lives underground. Oh, it was a magical land! How could they have missed it? Surely their god wouldn't blame them for enjoying it.

Or enjoying each other, wife or not.

And so, not-so-slowly, the world was repopulated with those who became known as Bacc'nalis, and the vibrant traditions carried on through generations, though the memory of the subterranean darkness—the grit of dirt, the stagnant air, the unrelenting darkness—was lost to time.

On the captain's orders, DeepService Team One let loose.

Dan set an alarm for an hour to avoid losing track of time, but when the alarm went off, nobody heard it.

The crew had followed the sounds of revelry to the city square, where the bulk of the dancing was taking place. Their bright clothes stood out against the naked and pulsating crowd, but Alice concluded that was for the best. They would need to find one another eventually, and she had no plans of letting these deadweights hold her back from getting caught up in the crowd.

The music was that of drums and voices from a stage on the edge of the square. Along the edge of the square ran long tables of refreshments.

Alice wasn't feeling especially hungry or thirsty, but before she knew it, the locals had swarmed her, pushing treats her way. "Thank—thank you. Yes, that looks— Ah, it tastes like pizza too. Oh, wonderful. Um, sure, I'll try it. Very— What? Oh, ha. Thanks, I love the boots too."

The sheer amount of offerings was making Alice claustrophobic, and she finally took her last bite of something that was melon-like in all ways except taste (it tasted like a pizza roll), and slipped away to get some dancing in.

The numbing tingle of her lips was always Alice's first sign that she was falling under the influence of a substance, and she grinned as it set in. She'd had to turn down the drugs from Queen Phet, but it looked like drugs had found her nonetheless. Nothing to be done about that but enjoy the ride. She let the pulse of the music take her away, accepted the slip and slide of the sweaty bodies around her. Maybe they knew she was there; maybe they didn't. It was all the same. *Everything* was all the same …

She'd never know how much time had passed before she spotted Vel in the crowd. It looked like the second-in-command was on the same high, whether she intended to be or not.

While Vel was all business normally, it didn't shock Alice to see her letting loose. One of her closest friends in college was the exact same way. Straight As, scholarship, volunteering … until Friday night. Then all bets were off.

Two Bacc'nali women had Vel pinned between them when the lieutenant caught her captain staring. She waved. Alice waved back. The two of them kept on dancing.

But slowly, breathing was becoming more of an ordeal as the crowd pressed in around Alice, and she had to throw a few elbows to free up enough space for her lungs to expand. And boy, was the jumpsuit cumbersome. Sweat-drenched, it stuck to her nooks *and* her crannies.

And then a thought crept in: how long had they been at this party? Had it been more than an hour? Dan said he was keeping track, but this felt like more than an hour.

Dammit! Why was she thinking about this? Couldn't she let herself have fun and leave it to Dan to keep track?

Where was Dan, though?

Almost as soon as she'd thought it, she felt something hard poking against her back. "Dan!"

"Alice! Hey, didn't see you there."

"Is the hour up?"

"Huh? Oh, don't worry about *that*. You want a drink?"

She stopped dancing and stared at him. This was all kinds of sideways. "I don't *want* to worry about it, Dan, believe me. But we do have a time constraint here."

"You know what?" he hollered above the roar of the music. "I'll go grab us both a drink. You stay here."

He tunneled away through the crowd, but Alice didn't stay put. Instead, she went searching for Caid. Could a hologram get drunk?

She caught a glimpse of him through the crowd, at the edge of the square, and shouldered her way over.

Caid was listening to a Bacc'nali woman pour her heart out to him, his head slightly tilted, his lips forming a gentle and sympathetic pout, as Alice approached.

Two males were trying their best to grab him in inappropriate places. However, by the time Alice reached him, those two had given up and simply started grinding on each other. All the while, Caid never took his eyes off his conversation partner. Or was it his client now?

Alice was about to announce herself when she paused. Perhaps it was rude to interrupt this session. Before she could decide one way or another, a hand gripped her shoulder and she turned.

"There you are!" Vel said, grinning broadly.

"Here I am."

"This is *so* fun!"

"Yes." But Alice was feeling less and less enthusiastic by the second. How unfair. Why couldn't she keep the buzz?

A strand of Vel's dark hair had snuck free of the ponytail

and was sweat-slicked to her forehead. She brushed it away with the back of her wrist, and the clumsy movement made it clear just how intoxicated she'd become. "You and me, we started wrong," Vel said. "I feel like we started wrong."

Alice began looking for an escape. There seemed to be only one place she could go to get away from the spiraling collapse of her team, and that was back onto *Emergence*. But the ship wasn't exactly close.

"Are you mad at me?" Vel asked.

"What?" Alice snapped her attention back to her second-in-command. "No."

"Oh. I was mad at you. I use to hate you. But I don't now."

"You *used to* hate me? What the hell, Vel? You say that like it was a long time ago. We met, like, twenty-four hours ago."

"I thought you were a cocky idiot," Vel continued. "I thought you weren't even qualified to lead a family of four to their booth at the back of a restaurant, let alone lead DeepService Team One on this mission."

Alice merely stared.

"But now? Now I think you have some good ideas. This. This was a good idea. This is fun. I'm having fun. A couple of Bacc'nalis invited me back to their home. I should go? I think I'm gonna go."

"No," Alice said, surprising even herself. "No, I don't think you should go. Vel, this might be getting a little out of control."

"Lighten up"—Vel hiccupped—"Captain. Hey. Hey." She tapped Alice's chest to get her attention, but at no point had Alice looked away from her. "I don't usually let myself have fun. This is nice. This is fun. I didn't have fun much when I was young. I was never good enough for my parents, and—"

"Caid!" Alice hollered. "Caid, I think we need you over here!"

The hologram extracted himself from his new client and appeared beside them. "Everything all right? You two bonding?" Vel bobbed her head, and he grinned. "Oh, that's great."

"No," Alice said. "She wants to talk about her parents. I think that's more *your* kind of thing."

Vel poked Alice in the chest again, hard. "You. I want to talk to you about my parents. I was never good enough. No matter what I did. I couldn't win."

Alice thought of the last time she'd spoken to her parents. Years ago. She put it from her mind quickly. "Yeah, happens to us all."

"*There* you are," said an out-of-breath Dan, grinning at his captain. Then his grin faded as he noticed the other two, and he looked down at his hands. "Oh no, I only brought two drinks. I didn't know we were all meeting back up again." He held out one of the smooth stone mugs to Alice, but Vel intercepted it and tossed it back.

Dan watched her then offered the remaining one to Alice. She reached for it, not to drink it but to keep Vel from taking another. But before she could, Dan's head snapped back in a splatter of dark blood, and the weapon blast echoed through the square half a heartbeat after.

CHAPTER
TWELVE

"Dan!" Alice shouted, leaping forward to catch him. But she knew it was too late. The concentrated blast had entered through an eye socket and blown the back of his head clear off. There was no coming back for the guy. Her 'dillo friend was roadkill.

At least, that was what happened in *almost* every reality.

But not the one our story follows.

In this reality, it went like so:

Dan held out the remaining drink to Alice, but a highly improbable thing happened. Vel grabbed the armadillo man by his yellow shirt collar and yanked him roughly in for a kiss.

A split second later, a Bacc'nali man directly behind Dan took a bullet to his third leg. The sound of the shot was closely followed by the unlucky man's howl as he went to the ground.

Alice didn't bother looking for the source of the shot. While she hadn't absorbed much of the academics in her life, her school years in Texas had taught her this much: it was almost impossible, in the heat of the moment, to locate the direction of a shooter.

"Get down!" Alice shouted, dragging Vel to the ground with her. She looked around to make sure the others had followed orders and found Dan glued in place, still on his feet.

He didn't move. He couldn't. All he could do was convulse.

"Fucking jitters," Alice growled before she jumped up, grabbed him by the shoulders, and took him to the ground with her. She didn't bother with Caid. If she couldn't grab his ass, it was safe to say he couldn't be shot. Best to use him as a diversion.

Vel's eyes widened when the next blast rang out. "They're trying to shoot us."

"No shit." Alice's school training was in full swing now. "Help me get Dan out of the way until he stops shaking." Then, staying low, the two dragged their convulsing crewmate toward the closest refreshment table.

The delayed reaction of the crowd began to kick in, and Alice grunted as the Bacc'nalis scrambled, their legs clipping her as she hunched over. A knee caught her in the rib, and she grunted, went to the ground, but got up again. She had no choice. If ever there was a "game time," an active shooter and an alien stampede was it.

She determinedly stayed low until all three of them made it beneath one of the large stone tables on the periphery. She listened, closing her eyes, but didn't hear any further blasts.

"I think they were shooting at us," Vel breathed. Then, turning her head away from the still-convulsing Dan, she vomited.

"Yeah, Vel," said Alice, "I think you might be onto something. And based on Dan's reaction, we're lucky to be alive. We need to keep moving, though. We may have these little blasters, but I ain't got a goddamned idea where to aim. Firing back is just giving up our position." She peeked out from behind the edge of the table and saw the stampede thinning. "Once the crowd is gone, we'll be easy to spot."

"Where should we go?" Vel asked.

Since Alice didn't know of any elementary school classrooms nearby where they could crawl into a corner and stay silent with the lights out, she was *almost* out of ideas. This was as far as her years of training took her. She'd have to rely on her critical thinking from this point on, and that was never a good sign in a crisis.

"We have to get back to the ship," Alice concluded. "Dan."

His convulsions had almost ceased, but he looked exhausted. His head lolled from side to side. "Ship," he whispered.

"I know. We gotta get back to the ship," said Alice.

"No," Dan murmured. "Ship. Bring the ship."

"Oh," said Alice. "*Oh.* Yes, do that!" She paused. "How do we do that?"

Vel touched a fingertip to her ear. "Allura. No, stop calling me that."

Alice snickered.

"We need you here. Now."

Alice's brows pinched together. "Wait, you have an earpiece? Why don't I have one?"

"You could've grabbed one." Sobering rapidly but by no means entirely sober, Vel hiked up her jumpsuit leg and pulled out her small blaster.

The town square had almost completely cleared out, and where the stampede had gone wasn't any of Alice's business, as far as she was concerned. What cover the chaos had given them was now lost.

But it also meant there was room for *Emergence* to land. If they sprinted their fastest …

A single glimpse of the shaky Dan and intoxicated Vel was enough to thwart those hopes.

Caid appeared beside her. "Is he okay?"

"No," Alice snapped. "But none of us are right now. Except maybe you."

The ship was so quiet that Alice wouldn't have noticed it landing if it hadn't temporarily blocked out the light on the other side of the square.

Even though she had no clue how they would make it there, seeing the port of *Emergence* open for them emboldened her to believe they could somehow figure this out.

"We're gonna have to make a run for it," Vel said.

"Ain't a chance in hell that'll work. Not with Dan like he is, and you … Ain't gonna work. Not even with the peashooters."

Vel turned to Caid. "You go first. They might not know you're a hologram. We'll see if they're still waiting for us."

Alice pointed at her. "Great idea. Caid?"

"I'll be emotionally honest with you: it'll hurt my feelings immensely if someone I don't even know tries to shoot me."

Alice's eye twitched. "That's a price I'm willing to pay."

Caid crawled from behind the table, puffed out his chest, and strode toward the gaping port of *Emergence*.

The stones exploding at his feet made it abundantly clear that the threat was still active.

Caid clutched his hands to his heart and shook his head with disappointment before continuing on to the ship.

"What now?" Alice asked, but Dan was already on it.

"Allura."

"You have an earpiece too?" Alice demanded. "Why did no one tell me we could wear them off the ship?"

"Locate a heat signature of the threat and send one their way ..." Dan groaned. "No, not like that. You know what I mean. *Shoot at them.*"

A moment's pause, then a spray of light shot from the side of *Emergence*. As the roof exploded on a nearby building, Dan yelled, "Now!" and the three of them dashed for it.

Halfway there, Dan's right knee buckled, but Alice grabbed him and hoisted him back to his feet. She felt the heat from a passing laser blast just miss her arm, and shouted into Dan's ear, "Allura! Help!"

Dust and pebbles from the second Bacc'nalian rooftop *Emergence* had annihilated rained down on the crew as they finally made it through the port and into the hangar deck.

"Allura!" Dan's voice wobbled. "Get us out of here! Nearest space fold, now!"

None of them spoke as the ship took off. Alice allowed herself a solid flop on her back while she caught her breath. Dan sat as well, but opted for slumping forward, his head between his knees. Vel stayed on her feet, but braced her hands on her hips, sucking air in through her nose.

"You're all ... sweaty," Allura 4000 murmured.

When they entered the bridge a few minutes later, Caid was waiting anxiously for them.

"Everyone okay?" the hologram asked. "No, of course you're not. I'll go set up our special space. Come see me once you've caught your breath." He hurried off to his room.

As the adrenaline subsided in Alice's limbs, she was

finally able to think. And the first thought that passed from her mind to her mouth was: "Did some fucker try to kill us?"

CHAPTER
THIRTEEN

Liz Windsor's flawless face filled the large screen on the bridge of *Emergence*. Her head appeared to float in a white void, and she seemed as calm as always, even a bit cheerful. Alice was determined to put an end to that.

"Hi, Liz Windsor. Um, yeah, care to give us any insight into why someone *tried to assassinate us?*"

She positioned herself closest to the screen, arms crossed, glaring, while Dan reclined in one of the nearby chairs behind her, continuing to recover from his jitters, and Vel planted her feet a step behind her captain, bracing herself against the spins that were setting in quick as the drugs and booze left her system. Caid hadn't returned from prepping his "special space," and Alice suspected he was crying or sulking or both.

The liaison forced a frown. "I'm not sure why you believe I would know."

"Because you know things, Liz Windsor. And the longer this mission goes on, the more I think we don't know diddly squat."

"I'm sorry you feel that way, Captain Luck."

Alice rubbed at her forehead. "Come on. Work with us. We're trying to make babies happen in space, and I can't for the life of me understand why someone *wouldn't* want that."

Liz Windsor pouted sympathetically. "You're sure that *you* were the targets of the attack?"

"Yes, *Liz Windsor*, I'm sure. We had to get Allura to unload on them so we could make it back to our ship. They rained bullets down on Caid, and that hurt his feelings! Who's *he* supposed to talk to about that when he's the only one on the crew who can even name more than four emotions!"

"I sense you're upset, Captain Luck. That is unsurprising, given your current vitals."

"How do you know about my vitals?"

"The suit reads them and sends them back to headquarters," Liz Windsor said flatly. "It wouldn't do for us to be unaware if one of our crew members died."

Alice narrowed her eyes at the screen. "Are you *expecting* that?"

"No. Is it possible that your current level of rage is related to the fact that you are one week past your ovulation window?"

"What? No! I'm pissed off because, *silly me,* I thought leaving Earth might mean I was safe from a mass shooting, but apparently not! Who the hell were they, Liz Windsor? Who doesn't like what we're doing?"

"There is always someone who does not approve of progress, Captain Luck. No mission worth pursuing can be completed without creating enemies."

Alice opened her mouth to speak, but before she could, Vel set a hand on her shoulder (mostly to steady herself) and stepped forward. "Do we have any intelligence to indicate this attack might have been carried out by the Alliance?"

Alice whipped her head around toward the lieutenant. "Who the hell is that?" When Vel didn't answer, Alice returned her attention to the screen.

Liz Windsor fidgeted slightly. "Your guess is as good as mine, Lieutenant Machiavelli, as I wasn't present for the action."

But Vel wouldn't be brushed off so easily. "It's well established that they don't feel kindly about the Depot. Have Depot crews experienced similar confrontations with them in the past?"

Liz Windsor looked as if she wouldn't answer. Her gaze shot toward something off screen, a paranoid little gesture. Then she said, "The previous crew might have had a few unpleasant run-ins with them, yes. Listen. I have full confidence that between the five of you, you're quite capable of handling whatever hostility might arise. And please don't forget that you're working under a time constraint. I'll let you regroup on your own now." Her plastic smile reappeared. "Very proud of you! Very proud!" And then the screen blinked off, and in its place was the vast expanse of space around their ship.

Alice inhaled deeply, her brain swirling with the disparate information. "Well. There's certainly a lot to unpack there."

Caid peeked into the bridge. "You need me?"

"Nope."

An idea hit.

"Actually, yes. Team meeting!"

"We're all here," Vel said.

"Perfect. Liz Windsor said something that's got me thinking ..." Alice paced back and forth in front of the window while the others looked on. "When I first heard about Caid and what he did, I thought, *Wow, what a useless crew member to have on board.* We only have four people, five if you include Allura."

"I like experiencing things in groups," said the operating system.

"Why would one out of the five—one-fifth, if you will—be here solely for mental health? *Unless* ..." Alice paused to build the suspense.

"Unless there was some facet of this job that was especially distressing to our mental health," Vel finished.

"Dammit, Susy. You gotta let me finish. But yes. That was where I was going. Now I ask you: How would Liz Windsor and the Depot know that without learned experience? And that brings me to my next question ..." She arched an eyebrow and smiled slyly.

"What happened to the last crew?" Vel said.

"Sweet Jesus. Who hurt you, Susy? Can't you let your captain speak?" Alice sucked air into her lungs, regaining composure. "But yes, that was my question. And I think I know who has the answer."

"Allura," said Vel, "what happened to the last crew?"

Alice grunted, but allowed the system to respond.

In the dulcet tones Alice was coming to love, Allura replied, "They all went mad and went missing in deep space. *So* deep inside it."

Silence fell over the bridge as Alice looked from Dan, who hugged himself, to Vel, who looked ready to fight that sentence, to Caid, who leveled a kind but sad look at his captain.

"Did you know this?" Alice demanded.

Caid bowed his head somberly. "Yes. I was aware of the

previous crew's medical history prior to embarking on this trial mission."

Alice waited for him to continue, and when it was clear he had no plans of that, she said, "And?"

"And what?"

"And what was the crew's medical history?"

"Oh. I can't disclose that."

Alice clenched her fists. "Only a man who physically couldn't be kicked would have the balls to play that card in this situation." She took a step closer to him anyway. "I don't know much about this intergalactic stuff, Caid, but I'd guess there's no HIPAA in outer space."

"You're right," he conceded. Then, putting his hand over his heart, he said, "It's more of a me thing. It wouldn't feel right telling you the things I was entrusted with. How could you trust me to keep your own personal thoughts and feelings private then?"

"That presumes I'd share those with you, *Caid*. And if someone shoots me, I won't be around to divulge the goodies! Don't you want the goodies?"

"I'll take all the goodies you can—"

"Allura! Subservience mode!"

Vel, meanwhile, who'd been thinking along other lines of blame, finally gave voice to them. "I can't believe you convinced us to let our guard down."

Alice turned toward her lieutenant. "Huh? Who are you talking to?"

"We're hired to be professionals, Captain. But under your orders, we acted like buffoons, and it nearly cost us our lives, let alone the mission!"

"Whoa, whoa, whoa … I didn't *make* you get shithoused, Susy. I just told everyone to have a good time. It's entirely possible to dance and grind while sober. Sure, it's weird, but it's not impossible."

"You're right," Dan said, and Alice was relieved to have a little backup against the smoldering glare Vel was sending her way. But then Dan continued: "Our captain put us in harm's way. I behaved like a fool. We should've died. I *should* have died. And if my jitters were any indication, I *did* die in the majority of realities. Your orders got a bunch of parallel mes killed today."

He pushed himself up from his chair to square off as Alice stared at him through a haze of confusion. "I don't know what any of that means, Dan. If I'm being honest, I still don't understand the jitters thing. If they were versions of you in another reality … then they're not real."

"They're real!"

Vel moved to stand shoulder to shoulder with Dan. "Permission to retire to our chambers, Captain."

Alice curled her lip in disgust. "For shit's sake, Susy. Do you have to be all procedurally correct when you mouth off to me? Fine. Yeah. Go to your rooms."

As Dan and Vel departed to sober the rest of the way up in peace, Alice stomped over to a large bucket seat facing the front window and plopped down.

Facing the empty expanse, she wondered briefly how any of this had happened. She glanced over at the timer. Twenty-two hours left. She was no stranger to time crunches. Procrastination was second nature to her. Sometimes she even met her deadlines. But this was no group project or birth of her first nephew; she doubted she could talk anyone into delaying the due date because she had put off her part of things.

"What am I going to do?" she muttered. In a place where the possibilities were literally infinite, where she had more places to run to than she could ever dream, she was stuck. She didn't know much about the Depot, but she suspected they could find her wherever she went. She'd have to take an escape pod to leave, and that would be easily trackable. She didn't know enough about how things worked out here in the universe to make an escape.

She was up against it now.

From behind her, Caid said, "You look like you could use someone to talk to."

Alice shut her eyes and bowed her head. "Fine. You win this round."

<h1 style="text-align:center">CHAPTER
FOURTEEN</h1>

"I tell you all the worst things I've ever done and we call it a day?"

Caid's office had been rearranged with two hammocks on stands in the center. Alice reclined in one, looking up at the synthesized night sky she'd learned by heart on Earth, and Caid Sonorian reclined in the holographic version beside her.

It was inarguably easier to talk this way. It reminded Alice of the nights she'd spent by a bonfire on the Boyd family ranch. Her neighbors had become famous (or notorious, depending on if you asked the teenagers in attendance or their parents who had to discipline said teens) for hosting all-out hootenannies around a big open flame. It was during one of those late, unsupervised bonfire nights that Alice had experienced her first kiss. It was also where she had her first acid trip, and where she first saw blue jeans completely engulfed in flames.

The Boyds had hammocks set up for a while, and Alice used to get there early to claim one for her own. So many nights staring up into the starry sky, talking about life, the universe, and hog wrestling.

She'd loved those hammocks. It was a shame the Boyds had destroyed them after Mary Boyd got knocked up in one her freshman year of high school.

"This isn't a confessional, Alice," crooned Caid, "but if you have things to get off your chest, of course I'll hold space for them."

"I can say anything and you won't be weird about it?"

"This is a safe space."

She tucked her hands behind her head and crossed her feet at the ankles. "I still want nothing more than to bone you."

True to his word, Caid didn't make it weird. "And how does that make you feel?"

"It annoys me. How else should it make me feel?"

"It makes you feel however it makes you feel. There is no 'should' with feelings."

"Jesus," Alice muttered.

"Does the idea of letting your feelings simply be, without judgment, resonate with you?"

Alice puffed out a laugh. "No. But I bet it resonates with a poster on the wall of a school counselor's office."

A shooting star raced across the ceiling.

"You say you want to engage in sex with me," Caid continued. "Why do you think that is?"

"Um." She considered it. "You're hot, I'm horny?"

"You don't think my position of authority has anything to do with it?"

"Authority? Caid. Come on. I'm the captain. You're just the sexy mind nurse."

He was unmoved by the jab. "Tell me, Alice, do you feel like a captain?"

She opened her mouth, but something inside her kept the words from spilling out, and she did something she almost rarely did.

She thought before she spoke.

"No," she said. "I don't. I honestly can't figure out why I'm in charge. Do you know?"

Caid was silent for a moment while the shadow of a nighthawk passed across the moon. "Yes, I know why. But I think it's important that you learn the reason for yourself."

"But … there is one?"

Caid chuckled. "There's more than one."

"And they're, you know, *good* ones?"

"I believe so."

It was the first genuine shot of relief Alice had felt since this ship took off, and she allowed herself to shut her eyes and pretend she was back at the Boyd ranch, the smell of cedar smoke soaking into her jeans and hair, a cool breeze like a feather over the exposed skin of her arms.

"Your case file says you're the youngest of seven children. Six older brothers."

"Mm-hmm …" In her mind's eye, Lex Boyd had challenged Jacky Harrison to a wrestling match in the field. Jacky always whooped his ass, and he never could get over it.

"When you cried as a child, what response were you met with by the adults around you?"

Alice's eyes shot open. "The hell? What do you mean?"

"What happened?"

"No clue. If I ever tried it, I don't remember."

"You weren't ever injured or sad?"

"Injured, sure," Alice conceded. "Slipped while hopping a metal fence once. Came down hard on it between my legs. Broke my pelvis."

"And you cried then, I assume."

"Nah. Not really the crying sort of injury. It knocks the wind out of you, and if you can get a holler in there before you pass out, you're considered a trooper. Charlie and Buck said I got a holler in, but I don't remember it."

"Interesting. So, when you encountered that great amount of pain, you didn't have to stay in it for long?"

"I guess not. Woke up in the hospital a few hours later. Got some of the best drugs of my life in those months that followed. And my brothers babied the shit out of me. I figure they were all glad it wasn't them. It hurt bad enough *without* adding in the extra sensitive bits they got."

"What about emotional pain?"

"Nah, no thanks."

"Hmm ..."

Alice hadn't heard him make that noise before, and she rolled her head toward his hammock. "What do you mean, 'hmm'? What's that about?"

"Oh, I find it interesting that you think you can simply say 'no thanks' to pain and it won't find you anyway."

Alice scoffed. "Okay." She sat up. "Hey, this has been great, as usual, but I need to do some research on Bacc'nali anatomy. You know, more than I unwittingly did down there today." She stood. "But before I head out ... The last crew? What was their deal?"

Caid threw his feet over the side of the hammock to face her. "You know I can't tell you that, Alice. I wish I could."

"But they're dead now?"

"Yes."

"That blows."

He pressed his lips together, and beneath the starlight, she thought she saw a tear glisten on his cheek. Damn, he was a softie.

"Do you worry you're going to fail on this mission?" he asked.

She opened her mouth, and for the second time, she paused to think before she spoke. "Yeah, I guess so."

"Good. I think you should spend a few minutes in the hot tub in your room imagining what would happen if you failed."

"Ew. Why? So I can have a panic attack?"

"You think sitting with the worst-case scenario for five minutes will send you into a panic attack?"

"Of course not. I could handle it if I had to. But I don't see the point of it. Why waste time on that?"

"How much time do you think Dan and Vel are putting toward considering the worst-case scenario right now?"

"Dan? Probably *all* of his time. Maybe Vel, too. She's probably getting off on all the scenarios where I screw up and get us all killed so she can say 'I told you so' in the afterlife."

"And do you think that's their burden to carry? After all, they're not the captain. They're not responsible for the life-or-death decisions."

Alice held up a hand. "Alright, alright. I get what you're saying. I'll take this a little more seriously. I might even read the full brief this time around."

Caid's eyes remained glued to her. "Okay, Alice. You know where you can find me. Any time you need. For what it's worth, I want to see you succeed in this mission. I like you."

Alice, who was already making for the door, paused with a foot hovering in the air. She looked back over her shoulder. "Like me as in ...?"

"I like you as a person."

"So not like … you do things, I watch?"
"What things?"
"Never mind. My mistake. I'll show myself out."

CHAPTER
FIFTEEN

Alice was getting the hang of DeepCUT *Emergence*. The ship could fetch her whatever she needed. She didn't have a clue how that worked, and it definitely felt like one of those questions that was better left unasked.

When she'd requested an apron, a candy-apple-red one had appeared out of a drop slot, and she tied it around her turquoise jumpsuit. When she'd asked for eggs, a carton of those appeared in the same slot near the kitchen wall on the bridge.

By the time Dan and Vel emerged from their rooms the following morning, whatever that meant in space, the meal was ready and laid out for them on the table. "Ta-da!"

Vel narrowed her eyes at the spread, and Dan, dressed in an oversized *Escape from New York* T-shirt and acid-washed jeans, yawned and asked, "What is it?"

"Well," said Alice, herding them toward the table, "it's a hearty breakfast, of course. I figured y'all might be a little hungover from yesterday—which we don't need to bring up again—so I started thinking about all the mornings on Earth where I woke up with a hangover and needed to rally quickly for an exam or church or one of those noon games at Kyle Field. And this is it—behold! The traditional Texas breakfast!"

Dan was looking more interested by the second. He sat himself closest to the pile of scrambled eggs.

"What's that?" Vel pointed to a stacked plate.

"Bacon. Or something like it. Do they not have that in your parallel universe? Sheesh. Well, for your sake, I'm glad you're here now." She wiped her hands on her apron. "I'll be honest, I still don't understand how this drop slot thing works. I assume the ship wasn't, like, teleporting in a pig. I can't imagine that would go well."

"The proteins of raw bacon strips were re-created based upon a blueprint," Allura explained.

Dan sat up straight and looked around for the omnipresent voice. "Whoa. She didn't even make it weird. I guess today might not be a disaster after all."

Alice waved it off. "I told her if she sexually repressed herself for the next couple of hours, I'd give her some keywords to find the good porn. Anyway, we've got bacon, eggs, sausage, tortillas, Texas toast, cheese grits, and some salsa verde to put on your eggs for a little added fun."

Dan grinned down at the food. "Wow. I'm getting the full cultural experience, aren't I?" He rubbed his hands together greedily, surveying the land to see where he should start.

"Oh! And I almost forgot—fresh-squeezed OJ and coffee."

As she brought over the carafes and set them in the last remaining space on the table, Vel said, "This is going to take a lot of time to eat. Do Texans usually spend this much time eating in the morning?"

"When we're hungover, sure. We eat until we don't have the spins. It's called being an adult."

Dan helped himself to the meal without any further ado, and even Vel stopped asking questions once she'd tasted the first strip of crispy bacon.

When Caid entered the bridge, announcing that he'd had the most rejuvenating meditation session of the trip so far and expressing his hope that everyone slept perfectly soundly, neither Dan nor Vel noticed him.

But Alice did, and she didn't appreciate his knowing smile when she met his eye. It was clear he assumed that this Texas breakfast was nothing more than a ploy to keep the crew from being upset about the day before ... which it absolutely was. But it was *also* her way of taking care of the people she was in charge of, and that was something a captain did, right?

What Caid didn't know was that Alice had another trick up her sleeve, and only once the meal was finished and Dan and Vel were sipping on their coffee like a cigarette after a good lay did she hit them with it.

"So this one time when I was out in the field for my senior capstone," she began, "there was this prize cow. She came from great, expensive stock, and it was time to start breeding her. The rancher paid something like fifteen grand —that's a lot of Earth money—to breed her with one of the top bulls in Texas. He and the bull's owner gave it a go at the right time, and nothing happened. The cow didn't get pregnant. Sometimes that happens. But the rancher tried it again with the same bull. Still nothing. He was thinking about giving up and selling her, but the sunk cost was too much for him, I guess, because he went and brought in *another* bull to try it with. Still no dice."

While it was plain enough that her crew had no clue why

she was telling them this, they were at least listening (thanks, meat comas!), so she went on.

"My professor brought a few of us on to figure out what was the problem. The bessie had plenty of eggs. But we also found something else. Her levels of adrenaline and other stress hormones were *off the charts*. That's not something you can tell from looking at a cow—they generally seem pretty chill and they have those big, empty eyes. Anyway, we had to figure out what was stressing her.

"At first, we thought it might be that we'd come too soon after the last breeding attempt. Maybe being mounted was stressful for her. Maybe lesbian cows were a thing. Who knows, right? So, we loaded her up and brought her to another pasture to be around other cows, then we measured her stress hormones. Totally in the normal range for a cow. We tried it again, bringing her to visit a bull this time. Measured again, and nothing. Her stress was fine. She wasn't a lesbian, or at least it wasn't the idea of having sex with a bull that was specifically unappealing to her." Alice paused. "Come to think of it, she could've been bisexual and we wouldn't've known. Never learned a methodology for figuring that out …

"The point is that something was stressing her out, and it wasn't the other cows or the presence of a bull. Then one day, I was driving out to the rancher's property with a couple of my classmates, and the AC had gone out in the truck, so we had the windows down. As we approached the property, I heard some disturbing sounds, smelled some disturbing smells, and then saw a sign for a slaughterhouse. The thing wasn't but two miles from the pasture where our cow was living. And I thought, *Well, I'll be damned!*

"We didn't have a lesbian cow, we had a *sensitive* one. She must've heard or smelled the cows over at the slaughterhouse, and being that close to death was stressing her out. She sensed danger, and she wasn't wrong. I'm pretty sure she would've ended up there if we hadn't figured it out. As soon as they moved her to a property farther away from the slaughterhouse, boom! She got knocked up! Ta-da!"

Vel blinked. "Why would you tell us a story about a cow's feelings right after we ate so much beef sausage?"

"Ah, shit." Alice rubbed at the back of her neck, staring at the grease pool on her own plate. "Well, I don't think it was real beef. The bacon was synthesized, so—"

"The beef was real," Allura replied.

Dan tapped a finger to his lips. "You think the Bacc'nalis have elevated stress hormones?"

Alice shot him with a finger gun, glad to get back on track. "Bingo!"

"But why?" Vel said. "What's their equivalent of a living next to the slaughterhouse?"

"Susy," Alice said, leaning forward. "Think about how you felt this morning before I healed you with this nourishing breakfast. The Bacc'nalis don't live *near* the slaughterhouse. They live *in it*. It's a hell of a good time, sure, but even I need a break every once in a while to rehydrate. Can you imagine the stress their bodies are under partying all the time and eating pizza fruit and having combat sex? Now, I'm not known to turn down a good time, but if I were to tell you I wasn't a little bit afraid of being murdered each time *I* slept with a guy I didn't know that well, I'd be lying. And we don't even do the combat sex thing on Earth. Well, most of us don't." She paused. "Maybe it's different for the Bacc'nalis, though. Maybe their men don't like killing their women." She turned to Dan, calling upon his cultural knowledge.

"Huh? Oh. No, it's the same for the Bacc'nalis. Their rituals of sexual engagement often lead to the death of the female partner. Not always intentionally, though."

"Not sure the intention matters all that much," Alice said. "So maybe I'm onto something, eh? That's the theory I came up with, at least, so I started digging into their sample biometrics, and you'll never guess what I found."

"Elevated stress hormones," Vel said.

"Okay, maybe you will guess. It wasn't adrenaline or cortisol or any other compound I'd seen before, but it was their version of it. It's begun to change their brain in dramatic ways, and it's only been elevated for the last Bacc'nalian century, based on historical data. It makes me wonder what's changed. Dan? Any guesses?"

He considered it. "Probably the genocide."

"The … what?"

"The Bacc'nali genocide of the Tripti people. It happened under the rule of King Bollsa'oot."

Alice felt her left eye twitch. *Be mature,* she ordered herself. *You're the captain!* But she couldn't stop herself. "King … Ballsout?"

"Bollsa'oot. King Bollsa'oot the Seventh, technically."

Now her right eye twitched. "There were *six* before him?"

"Yeah, why?"

"Shouldn't we be addressing the genocide part?" Vel said. "That seems important."

Alice waved her hand. "Right, right. Tell me about the genocide of King Ballsout the Seventh." She sipped her coffee to hide the grin she couldn't possibly suppress.

"What is there to say about genocide, really?" replied Dan. "It started like every genocide starts: someone's father didn't love them."

"King Ballsout the Sixth, you mean?" Alice asked. The question was just a little something for her.

"No, King Ardon the Second."

Alice bit her lip and attempted to breathe deeply.

"The king wiped out the Tripti people," Vel said, taking over where her captain was unable to, "and that led to the partying?"

Dan shook his head. "Not right away. And the Bacc'nalis have always been a partying people. They descend from the survivors of a mass extinction event that—"

"I don't need the whole saga," Alice said, waving for him to skip ahead.

So he did. "The generation responsible for carrying out the genocide lived with the guilt and shame of it. The following generation hated their parents for it. The next generation started a movement to repair the damage their grandparents had done. Naturally, that didn't work, because their grandparents were still largely alive and didn't want to admit they were wrong. By the time the next generation came along, the great-grandchildren of the murderers, the kids were so tired of everyone moping and fighting and talking about the genocide, they thought it best to forget about it and move on. Queen Phet is among that generation. Her great grandfather was King Bollsa'oot. In an attempt to repair his reputation in the eyes of his daughter, Princess Orgyna, who hated him, King Bollsa'oot the Seventh declared the final day of the massacre a planetary holiday. Each year, they would throw a massive party to commemorate it, but it wasn't enough to repair his relationship with Princess Orgyna. So, he changed it from a day of celebrations to a week of them. Still not enough. The week became massacre month. By the time this generation came along, Queen Phet's generation, the party month was a way of life."

"And the reparations the grandchildren pushed for?" Alice asked. "They ever make up for the genocide?"

"Nope. They don't even talk about it. In fact, most Bacc'nalis alive today aren't even aware it happened."

"Damn," Alice said. "That's terrible. We've had a few of those on Earth, but no one forgets about them."

"You mean like the Cambodian genocide?"

"The what?"

"Never mind, Captain."

Alice stood from her chair. "Okay! Regardless of how the Bacc'nalis got themselves to where they are, we gotta get them out of the slaughterhouse. And I know exactly what they need for that. They need *boring*."

"And how are you going to do that?" Vel said. "You planning on changing their entire culture in a matter of hours?

"Nope. But I'm going to introduce something that will." Alice grinned at her crew. "Folks, we're gonna get some nerds laid."

CHAPTER
SIXTEEN

With the help of Dan's brain and Allura's database, it took almost no time at all to find another planet with a struggling birth rate that fit the bill.

And so, within a few short hours of travel by space folds, *Emergence* and her crew descended toward the planet known as Waff JFP990, or "Location" by the preeminent species.

"They speak English, right?" Alice said as the four of them waited in the hangar for touchdown.

"Of course," Dan said. "Very plain English."

"Perfect. And they know we're coming?"

"I informed the head of the association, yes."

"The association?"

"The global association."

"No king or queen or whatever?"

"Nope. Everything's done by committee."

Alice grinned because this was working out perfectly so far. "Sounds tedious."

She touched a finger to her earpiece. Now that she knew about these handy comm devices, she'd be damned if she missed out on an on-the-go direct connection to her favorite onboard computer. A jolt ran through her as she stared out the window at their destination. This was only her second alien planet, and the thrill of that hadn't worn off yet.

At a distance, Location glistened like an emerald. As they drew closer, a dense canopy emerged below them. The planet was covered in a tangle of lush jungle.

Allura found a slight break in the trees large enough to "fit it in," and after a flash of nothing but green all around them, they were finally below the treetops, where Alice could get a sense of the place.

As it turned out, the treetops extended hundreds of feet in the air, and there was plenty of space below them for an entire civilization to exist—quiet, sheltered, and unobtrusive.

It didn't appear that a single tree had been felled to make space, but rather the buildings accommodated the trees, snaking around them or simply using a massive trunk as part of the structure itself.

Alice turned to Vel. "I feel more relaxed already, don't you?"

The lieutenant stared fixedly through the window. "I believe it would be unwise to let my guard down around a race I've never met."

"Right. But you're, like, maybe a little bit more relaxed now?"

"Relaxing is a choice, and not one I've made yet, Captain."

From Alice's other side, Dan said, "I'm relaxed."

She patted him on the shoulder. "Thanks, Dan. You have weapons too, right?"

"Of course. Relaxed but heavily armed."

The ship lurched.

They'd touched down on Location.

"I'm glad you're feeling relaxed," Caid whispered in Alice's ear from behind her. A shiver ran down her spine, and though she knew it was impossible, she could practically feel his warm breath on her neck. "You're really stepping into this role, Alice. Good work."

She swallowed hard. "Shall we?"

Dan hit the button for the port hatch, and DeepService Team One walked out onto the foreign planet.

A group of aliens were waiting for them. The humanoids were dressed in what appeared to be burlap, but finely tailored burlap that fit their curves. In fact, they were *mostly* curves—specifically, one single curve.

The Jejoons were blobs of creatures. With their short limbs and round bodies, they reminded Alice of a young child's drawing of a human.

Each had large black eyes and a tiny mouth that was almost invisible, lacking anything quite like lips to set it apart from the rest of the face.

Alice leaned toward Vel. "It's probably not a big deal that *I* wouldn't have sex with one of them, right? Not even if my species' existence depended on it. Like, this isn't about my preferences, correct?"

"Exactly," Vel mumbled. "But for what it's worth, I agree with your sentiment."

"Welcome," said the burlapped blob in the middle of the greeting committee. "We are so glad you have come to visit."

A blob to the left added, "We have long discussed the merits of hiring the Depot to match us with a new species, but the proposal never made it through committee."

"Never made it *to* committee," said the head blob. "The debate over whether it was a responsible use of our funds has kept it off the table, even while our birth rate plummets."

DeepService Team One paused a few steps away from the hosts, and Alice stuck out her hand to shake (she'd cleared it with Dan before).

The head blob offered his soft, lumpy hand, and gave her a dead-fish shake that left her with a strong urge to kick him in the knee.

Man up, she thought. But then she put it from her mind and returned to the task at hand. "The good news for you is that our client will be covering the costs. I'm Captain Alice Luck, and this is my crew—Minister Dan Zone, Lieutenant Susy Machiavelli, and Doctor Caid Sonorian." Dan had advised her that titles mattered a great deal to these folks.

"Welcome," said the head blob. "My name is Fon, and I'm this week's head of the organizational committee of hosting. We are glad to assist you however we can. We spent the last hour preparing for your arrival and hope we accurately anticipated your needs."

"I'm sure you have," Alice said. Beside her, Caid placed both hands over his heart and thanked them with a gracious bow.

"Please follow us, and do let us know if we're walking too fast for you."

One of the blobs said, "Fon is known for his fast pace," and giggled.

Alice prepared herself to run, and even Vel was making sure all her gadgets were properly fastened to her jumpsuit, but when the committee turned and made toward the rest of the city, Alice felt inclined to ask if they were quite all right. The pace was so slow it called to mind the clock ticking down aboard *Emergence,* counting off the seconds until they failed this mission, lost the money, and were sent to the far reaches of space to die of boredom.

Alice knew exactly who would share her pain, and she looked to her second-in-command. But Vel was staring so intensely at the feet of the blobs, as if she could move them along with her mind, she didn't notice her captain at all.

Alice looked to Dan. If he was feeling impatience, he showed no signs of it. What a legend!

Then she remembered: in the brief, which she'd read slightly more than half of, it had said that the Jejoons didn't like to be hurried. In the moment of reading, the factoid hadn't quite lodged itself in her memory. She'd skimmed right over it, thinking, *I don't have time for this level of detail.*

But maybe she should have given it more consideration. So long as she and her crew were on a tight deadline, it was probably best not to involve a species whose speed made you want to tell a tortoise to slow down and lay off the amphetamines.

There was no way out of it now, though. They would have to endure the agonizing pain of unvocalized impatience.

Alice returned her attention to the city. It was getting no closer. She slid over to Dan. "This is taking too long," she whispered.

"There's nothing we can do. Slow, deliberate movement is part of their culture. One of their uniting values is 'hesitation,' so be grateful they've decided to move in the right direction at all."

"No," she said. "I refuse to accept that this is the only way we're going to move around here. This is literal torture. There has to be something we can do."

"There's nothing, Captain." He shut his eyes and held up his hands. "Please, be patient."

"Hard pass on that. I have an idea."

"Oh no."

"Don't worry, it's a great one. Halloween my freshman year in college, I dressed up as a slutty football referee. Part of the costume was these dominatrix boots with four-inch heels. Found them at a Goodwill and basically built the outfit around them. But they were hell to walk in. I kept getting left behind the group as we went from bar to bar. So, I picked out the dude of our group who I was pretty sure was still a virgin, and I told him, flat out told him, that he was now my helper. He gave me piggyback rides all over that night."

"What's a piggyback ride?"

She told him.

"Captain, no."

"Tell me, Dan, is there anything *specifically* in their culture that would frown upon this idea?"

He was about to protest, to shut the whole thing down and insist she focus her attention on her own patience instead of this plan, but the look in her eyes stopped him. She was going to do this one way or another. "Nothing specifically," he said. "They're accommodating, so tell them it's a custom where you're from for the guests to ... you know."

"Gotcha." She patted him on the back and found his plates pleasantly supple through his orange crew shirt. Weird.

"Fon," she said, easily stepping in front of the hosts. "I have a request to make of you."

"You are the guests. We will honor it if we can."

"Great. Where I come from, it's a custom to allow the guests on a new planet to carry their gracious and hesitant hosts on their backs for a little while. Would you allow

Minister Zone, Lieutenant Machiavelli, and myself to carry the three highest ranking of you on our backs the rest of the way to town?"

Fon's blobby center wiggled a little as he considered it. He looked to the others, and, magically, they each began to giggle.

As they sorted out who would take whom, Alice whispered to Vel, "Please don't be mad. I couldn't—"

Vel stopped her with a hand on the shoulder. "This is easily the best idea you've had all mission." And then she squatted down and let one of the Jejoons climb onto her back.

It was not a fantastic fit, anatomically speaking. The Jejoons' bodies were too round and their limbs too short to clasp on, but even with the difficulties, the group was able to triple their speed.

"My, my!" shouted Fon from Alice's back. "This is so exhilarating! I'm sure I'll regret the recklessness, but I can't wait to tell the others about this!"

CHAPTER
SEVENTEEN

There was a period of time between T=1234! and T=5678! when a small gathering of minds from around the multiverse met to discuss an insidious problem that had not yet been solved and was causing most of the problems throughout advanced civilizations.

The problem was this: decisions were always made too quickly or too slowly.

With no record of any decision made at a pace that felt neither rushed nor dragged out, this ragtag group turned to the one thing they trusted: math.

The decision to use math only came after an overly long discussion that left everyone with an increased sense of urgency to solve this pressing issue.

They began by bringing in nearly infinite data on the subject—all the decisions they'd each made, all the decisions their friends and family had made, all the decisions their governing bodies had made. And then they began the evaluation.

When they'd reach a crossroads on how to proceed, they would consider it, debate, feel like the decision was being dragged out, then decide on a way forward and add their decision to the data set.

In the end, they were able to plot it on a graph. It's always a step in the right direction once you can do this, with one type of exception, and of course this fell into that realm of exception.

They had not found a solution in any practical sense. Instead, in graphing their problem, they had discovered an asymptote. The curve of too slow never met the inverse curve of too quick. There was an infinite chasm between them.

Discouraged by their results, they decided to pursue a more realistic question, and began searching for the name of the force behind their wives leaving them.

Alice thought she was going to die. Every fiber of her body felt ready to tear itself free from the others. A shiver ran down her spine, but she suspected that was her nervous system trying to keep her conscious.

The crew of DeepService Team One sat at a large round table with no fewer than three dozen Jejoons in a dimly lit chamber built onto the side of an especially large tree trunk. This was the Decision Chamber, and Alice abhorred the irony. This was a place where decisions came to die. She'd only been there, what, an hour? And she already knew that much.

The discussion hadn't yet moved to anything relevant. The time had so far been spent in a calm gridlock over whether it was prudent to introduce a motion to introduce the topic of breeding with the Bacc'nalis.

Alice leaned close to Dan seated on her left. "You're armed with more than a peashooter, right?"

"Yes."

"Whatever I might say to you, don't let me have it."

He shot her a wide-eyed look.

On Alice's right, Vel sat straight as a board, her hands perfectly placed in her lap, unmoving, her eyes focused straight ahead.

Unbeknownst to the others, Vel was asleep. Her military training hadn't been intended for a situation like this, but tools were tools. Her subconscious was taking the night shift, and if anything seemed off, she would wake ready.

On the other side of Vel, Caid listened to the discussion intently, nodding empathetically with every single point made, regardless of whether it directly contradicted the one before it.

"How much time do we have left?" Alice muttered to Dan.

He checked the apparatus on his wrist. "Fourteen hours."

Alice jumped. "Are you shitting me?"

"Am I *shitting*?" said Dan. "Am I shitting ... on you? Er, wait. I don't understand the question. What's that got to do—"

"Guess that phrase didn't make it across the galaxy. Doesn't matter." She stood, and all eyes in the room turned (slowly) toward her. Vel snorted then blinked rapidly. "Fon," Alice said, addressing the blob that was clearly not in charge now that they'd entered the chamber. He hadn't said a word during the discussion. "Remember that feeling you experienced while riding on my back?"

He hugged himself shyly. "Yes. I remember it."

"What if I told you that you could feel that every day and nothing bad would happen?"

"Fon?" said the elder in charge. "What is our guest describing?"

"It was a rush of blood, Decision Monitor. My heart rate was … it was *elevated!*" Fon spat the last word defiantly, and a gasp left the rest of the Jejoons.

"You speak of recklessness, Fon," warned the decision monitor.

Then the blob Vel had transported spoke out of turn. "It's true, Your Intentionality. I, too, felt an elevated heart rate, and it was the most alive I've ever felt!" A blush filled her white cheeks.

"I don't want to rock your whole world," Alice said. "Eh, no, actually, I do. Your birth rates are low; have you considered why?"

"Yes, we've considered it fully," said the decision monitor.

"And?"

"And we've come to the conclusion that the decreasing birth rate is nothing to get worked up about. Yes, it will cause problems long term, but we can't act hastily and pick the wrong approach to remedy the situation."

"But do you know *why* babies aren't happening?"

"We have studied it in depth and believe we have a reasonable theory, but until it's properly reviewed and the results can be replicated the requisite twenty thousand times, we're not ready to decisively say."

"What is your theory, then?"

The decision monitor cleared his throat. "I will defer to the Manager of Careful Replication and Duplication for that."

"Fine," muttered Alice, looking around for who the hell she would need to shake down next.

A female blob cleared her throat. Alice waited. The female blob inhaled slowly. Alice shut her eyes and asked the multiverse for strength.

Finally, the manager of careful replication and duplication spoke. "The working theory—and again, I cannot stress enough that this has not completed our standards of rigorous verification—is that the problem we are encountering with birth rate is mostly behavioral."

Alice leaned forward. "Meaning?"

"Meaning it's related to our species' behavior."

Alice flopped back into her seat. "For chrissakes …"

Dan took over where his captain could not. "What specific behaviors are causing the infertility?"

"Oh, no, no, no," said the manager of careful replication and duplication, "there are no infertility issues detected."

"What behaviors are specifically contributing to the lack of offspring, then?"

"After examining tens of thousands of data sets, there were a few behaviors that looked like promising culprits. But ultimately, we ruled those out, as they were generally not within four standard deviations. However, one behavior was frequently reported, and we do believe that it might have something to do with the drop in birth rate, though as I've said, this still has not been properly vetted by our processes."

"What is it?" Alice demanded.

"It's not so much a behavior as a lack of one."

"Sweet baby Jesus," she breathed. "Would you please *tell us* what behavior was lacking in your unverified study?"

"Of course, but I don't know how much use you will get

from that knowledge. Unverified studies are hardly anything to act upon."

"Just ... humor ... us," the captain forced out through gritted teeth.

"Very well," said the manager of careful replication and duplication. "After our first few exhaustive studies, the one commonality we found among those who had partners but were without children was a behavioral one. And that behavior—or as I said before, the lack of it—was sexual intercourse."

"Sex?" Alice spat. "Wait, are you serious? Your birth rate is diminishing because no one is having sex around here? Wow, what a breakthrough!"

Dan gently touched her arm, and only then did she realize she was out of her chair again. She sat down. "Okay, so y'all aren't getting laid, and it's causing problems, right?"

Those around the table murmured in a tone that neither confirmed nor denied the claim.

"Why aren't you having sex?"

"Oh," said the manager of careful replication and duplication, "we haven't even *begun* to establish a framework for a study on that."

"Forget the study." When the blobs around the table gasped, Alice dialed it back. "Listen, I would love to hear why each of you are failing to have sex. I know it's personal, but it would be very helpful if we could conduct an impromptu survey."

"Not personal at all," said the decision monitor. "Sexual intercourse is merely a physical act that is necessary for producing offspring. There is little more boring or mundane than sexual intercourse."

"I think I found the problem," Vel mumbled before appearing to tune back out again.

Alice wholeheartedly agreed. "I love that there's no shame around sex for you, but … maybe we're talking about two different things here. What does sexual intercourse look like to you?"

"It's the same," Dan said. "They're talking about the same thing."

Alice looked around the table. "So the whole"—she made a circle with the thumb and index finger of her left hand and jabbed her right index finger through it a few times—"that's what you think is boring?"

"We have other things preoccupying us," said the decision monitor. "It is not that the act is not temporarily pleasurable, but I for one fail to remember to do it when I return home to my wife."

"And she fails to remember, too?"

"Oh yes, she's busy cleaning up my messes, carrying our emotional burdens, and keeping an eye out for signs of supernovas in nearby galaxies."

"Typical wifely duties," Dan said after a long moment, taking over while his captain was so obviously speechless. "But I ask you this: if your wife initiated sexual intercourse with you, would you turn her down?"

"Of course not."

"And let's say you did not have your wife. If a shapely woman of another species was interested in mating with you, would you turn her down?"

"Probably not. Of course, that would depend on—"

"Right, right," Dan said, finally growing impatient himself. "But if she wanted to do some strange things that would, uh, elevate your heart rate, would you turn her down?"

"I hardly see how I could," said the decision monitor. "This woman you describe seems proactive."

"Very."

Alice, asserting captain's privilege, took over. "Here's what we're going to do, and the best part about it is that you don't need to make any decisions. I'm going to tell you how it will happen, *capisce?* Oh wait, you probably don't know Italian. Um, understand?"

The decision monitor blinked his big, watery eyes. "We'll have to put it to a vote."

"No," Alice said. "No, you won't. I'm telling you right now what's going to happen. You're going to do as I say, and if anyone questions the procedures, tell them I bullied you into it." She paused, waiting for someone else to protest, but no one did. "Great." She grinned at Dan and Vel, and Caid gave her a supportive wink.

This was how a captain was supposed to be, wasn't it? Assertive, honest, clever.

"Now," she said, addressing the Jejoons, "will one of your males please give me some ejaculate?"

"Wow, Captain Luck, you took charge back there," Dan said, hurrying after her as the crew left the Decision Chamber and returned to the ship.

"You dominated them back there, Captain," Vel said. "I didn't know you had it in you."

"I hope you take a moment to tune into your body and see how this new approach feels," Caid added.

Alice allowed herself a satisfied grin but otherwise didn't have time to indulge in the flattery. Not while she hurrying to get the warm tube of pistachio-colored Jejoon ejaculate back to her lab. In an ideal world, which Location was not, she would've also had a sample of Jejoon eggs, but those were harder to extract, and time was running short.

As they marched aboard *Emergence*, Alice held the warm vial in the air, announcing, "I have jizz!"

"Well done, Captain," Allura said.

Alice stopped in her tracks, feet away from the glass elevator. "Wait. I said … and you aren't gonna … Allura, I already gave you the good search words." She turned to Dan, Vel, and Caid a few steps behind her. "Either of y'all know how to run a diagnostic check on the system?"

"Maybe you made it too easy," said Vel.

"Correct," said Allura. "I like it *harder*."

Vel pointed to the ceiling. "Diagnostic check complete."

With that out of the way, the four of them loaded onto the elevator, then entered the bridge. "There's a lab in my room," Alice explained, and led the way.

The sample processing was instant once Alice inserted the tube.

On her screen popped up the word COMPATIBLE in black letters on a green backdrop. So far, so good. "Allura, can we tell anything from this sample as to whether or not it works the other way? Do we know if the Bacc'nali ejaculate would be a match with a Jejoon egg?"

"Not with total certainty. There exist DNA components of the Jejoon semen that go unused within the Bacc'nali eggs, which indicates that the Jejoon eggs might have additional requirements that the Bacc'nali semen doesn't meet for a healthy offspring."

Alice frowned at the screen. "And what are the odds that the mismatch would lead to, say, birth defects?"

"Roughly one out of every two hundred offspring of a Bacc'nali male and Jejoon female would be born with an extremely disfiguring genetic mutation."

Alice turned toward the others. "One out of two hundred ain't bad, right?"

If their expressions were any indication, it was very bad.

She turned back to the monitor. "What kind of mutations are we talking about here?"

"Mostly extra limbs," Allura replied.

Alice felt her spirits lift. "That's not so bad! One could argue that would be *useful*."

"Unfortunately, any extraneous limbs would be entirely useless, and there could be as many as thirty-one of them per individual."

She wasn't ready to give up yet. "That could be, uh … a status symbol, maybe?"

"I can provide a rendering for you."

Alice cringed. "Please don—"

Too late. It appeared on the screen.

"Quivering quasar!" Dan spat, jumping back.

Alice's hand flew up to her mouth. "Sweet baby Jes— No, no, no …"

"Kill it!" Vel shouted.

"I'll go set up my room," Caid said, scurrying off.

"Get it off the screen!" Dan yelled, and Allura did as she was told.

The lab fell densely silent.

The mutations were not ideal, Alice had to admit.

Her heart still racing, she squeaked, "Allura, how much time do we have left?"

"Roughly ten hours, Daddy."

Alice bowed her head, inhaled deeply to steady herself, then spun on her heels to face her crew. "Great. Once we get Queen Phet to sign off on mating with the Jejoons, we might even have time to spare."

CHAPTER
EIGHTEEN

Queen Phet's face appeared on the giant screen at the helm of the bridge. "I assume you have good news?"

Backed up by her crew, who were hopefully not visibly cringing at what she was about to say, Alice rolled her shoulders back. "Great news, Your Majesty. Not only do I believe we've found the cause behind the Bacc'nali infertility, but we've made contact with a species who is biologically compatible and should remedy the situation."

"Oh, delightful! Who are they?"

"The Jejoons, Your Majesty."

"Never heard of them."

"That's because they're boring as mud, but you're going to love them. And I know they will love you and your people."

"Apologies, Captain. Did you say they were *boring*?"

"Quite vanilla."

Queen Phet narrowed her eyes. "That doesn't sound like fun."

"Then allow me to point out that their dullness means

you will absolutely get to have your way with them, and it will blow their mind."

Dawning comprehension crept onto the face of the queen until she broke out in a grin. "Yes, that might be a nice change of pace. They won't have seen any of my people's famed tricks."

"Your Majesty, from what I've seen of their planet, lady-on-top is enough to rock their world. May we bring an envoy?"

"Oh, absolutely!" said the queen, clapping her hands excitedly. "Bring me their finest, best-endowed male."

"Yes, Your Majesty. Right away."

Alice turned back to the crew after the final sign-off, once the screen returned to being a window. "I think we could probably grab any of the Jejoons to bring along. She won't know the difference."

"You don't worry that she'll find out and report her dissatisfaction to the Depot?" Dan said.

Vel added, "You made a promise to her, Captain. We ought to do our best to fulfill it."

Alice held up her hands. "Great. We have less than ten hours to wrap this up or else we don't get paid and they shoot us off to Planet Boresville, but you're right—we need to stage some sort of worldwide search for the biggest schlong. Wow, I still can't understand why you're not the captain, Susy."

"Is it possible," said Dan, cautiously inserting himself into the tension, "that the Jejoons already know who has the largest penis?"

Alice glared at him. "Like a *registry*? You're asking if I think they might have a dick registry?"

Dan held up his hands. "Well, it does sound silly when I hear it back."

Alice made for the elevator. "Let's get a move on. We'll grab whatever male is trying to compensate the least and doesn't have a wife, and then we'll take him back to Bacc'nalia and get him laid." She tossed a look over her shoulder to find her crew in the same place. "Hop to, y'all! We're doing the Lord's work here!"

"He has a wife as well," said the decision monitor.

Inside the Decision Chambers, Alice pinched the bridge of her nose. She'd been going around the large table, pointing to a Jejoon, and asking the same question, over and over. "Can you please tell me who *doesn't* have a wife?"

"Many of our people," said the decision monitor.

Alice's skin crawled. "Which one? Just one. We only need one. Please, point me to one!"

"The manager of careful replication and duplication does not have one."

"A male, Decision Monitor! She is a she!" Alice turned to Vel. "Am I a ghost? Why do they not hear the words I'm saying?"

Vel took over. "All females must leave the room right now."

The Jejoons blinked.

"Dan." Alice turned to the minister of weapons and culture and didn't bother to lower her voice. "You got any guns on you? I feel like diplomacy is failing fast."

The female Jejoons quickly wobbled from the room.

"Great," said the captain. "Now if you have a wife, leave the room."

Everyone else stood to leave.

"Hold the hell on! *All* of you have wives?"

The decision monitor nodded. "Yes. It is a requirement to sit on this committee."

"What about the women?"

"They have wives as well."

"They're all lesbian blobs?"

The decision monitor steepled his fingers beneath his chin. "I'm not sure what a lesbian is."

Dan intervened. "Hold on. When you say 'wife,' could a male Jejoon also be a wife?"

"Of course."

Alice had thrown a cheap punch before. It was fifth grade, and Shelley Dillinger wouldn't stop chanting, "Itty-bitty titty committee!" on the playground while pointing straight at Alice's chest. The boys were starting to notice, and nothing Alice said would make the little twerp knock it off. Hence: fist time.

But the frustration she'd felt that day on the playground had nothing on what she felt in the Decision Chamber on Location in that moment. "Will you *please* direct us to the nearest male Jejoon who does not have a wife?"

The decision monitor began, "I'll have to run it by—" then pulled up short.

Ah, he's learning, thought Alice. Maybe she wouldn't have to deck him.

"Are you telling me I must do it under threat of harm?" he asked.

Alice grinned. "If that's what you're into. Now lead the way."

Finally, he did, and Alice, who'd forgotten how slow they moved, immediately explained about the piggyback thing, then off they all went, DeepService Team One crew and the decision monitor, out into the quaint city streets beneath the tall canopy.

"What's your name?" Alice asked her hitchhiker, figuring polite conversation might be called for so long as he was pressed up against her back.

"Pon."

"Pon?" she asked, wondering if she'd misheard and had accidentally grabbed Fon instead.

"Correct. Pon. My, you do move quickly! I can feel the wind against my skin, and it's a still day! Take the next left up here." His grip on her tightened as he braced for the corner.

Centripetal forces gave Alice no problems as she turned left. "Pon, do you have a last name?"

"Pon."

"Pon Pon?"

"Correct."

"Should I even ask about a middle name?"

"If you wish. I have two."

"And they are?"

"Jon Mon. Next right! Coming up quick." It was not.

"Pon Jon Mon Pon is your name?"

"Yes. But do you think it wise to speak while you move so quickly?"

Alice felt pretty comfortable with her ability to manage both—after all, God gave her these tree-trunk thighs for something, though she never expected it would be this—but she was also happy for the conversation to end.

They arrived at the door of a wifeless Jejoon, and Alice was forced to help steady Pon Jon Mon Pon as soon as she set him down.

Grinning wildly, he clutched at his chest. "My heart rate is elevated."

"Great. This the place?"

"Yes."

"What's this guy's name?"

"Don Won."

"Oh, that's … perfect. Cool. Let's say hello."

Pon rubbed his hands together anxiously. "But I didn't provide customary warning ahead of time. We will need to do that first."

Alice looked to Dan, who shrugged helplessly.

"Fine," she said. "How do we do that?"

"We should write our request down and leave it on his doorstep. When next he decides to leave his house, he will find it. Then it will be his turn to write us a—"

Alice knocked on the door. "Don Won! Open up." She counted to five, then knocked again. "Don Waaaaaaaaahn! Your world needs you!"

When the door cracked open, only a single watery eye could be spotted through the narrow space. "This is highly unusual," said a small voice. "Pon, do you know this woman?"

"I do, Don. She is very important. But also, she has made all of this happen against my will. It's best you listen to her and do what she says."

"Do you have the committee's backing on this?" Don asked.

"Yes—they are all being bullied by her too."

"A bully! On Location? Very well, then. Committee knows best. I will allow myself to be bullied, too." He opened the door farther. "What is it that you ask of me, bully woman?"

"My name is Captain Alice Luck with DeepService Team One. We have been sent here by the Depot on behalf of Queen Phet of Bacc'nalia. They are a dying breed, but we believe the Jejoon people are a perfect sexual match. And since your planet finds itself in a similar situation, we hope to bring an envoy to meet the queen and reproduce. That's where you come in. Tell me, Don Won, would you like to take a queen as your wife?"

The little blob considered it, blinked. "No thanks. She doesn't sound very useful. And can she even predict supernovas? I should think not. A queen isn't worried about anything like that."

Pon inched closer to Alice and whispered, "Bully him. He'll do it."

Alice shot the blob a sideways glance. It wasn't the worst idea she'd heard that day. "Don Won, you're coming with us. The fate of your planet depends on it, as does the fate of another planet, as does the fate of my crew. Susy."

She turned toward her second-in-command, ready to order the woman to be the piggy upon whose back Don Won would ride …

But Vel wasn't there.

"Huh." Alice spun a full circle, stopping at Dan. "You see where she went?"

Dan shook his head.

"Caid? You happen to notice Susy sneaking off?"

The hologram stroked his chin and inspected the captain. "The term 'sneaking off' carries with it a sense of suspicion and mistrust, Alice. We should circle back to it later on when we have a quiet moment. No, I don't believe she sneaked. I don't know where she went, but I'm going to give her a generous assumption. Perhaps she understood that she needed a minute for herself and went back to the ship for self-care."

"That doesn't sound like her." Alice tapped at the device in her ear. "Allura, can you hear me?"

"Yes, Daddy," came the silky-smooth voice.

"Is Susy back on the ship?"

"No, Daddy. Would you like me to connect you to her comms?"

"Ooh! Yes, please."

"You are now connected."

Alice turned her back to the others, pressing her finger against the earpiece. "Susy? Where are you?" She waited. No response. "Susy? Susy, can you hear me? Vel!"

Still nothing.

"Allura, why isn't she responding? Could her comms be busted?"

"What is it?" whispered Dan, but Alice waved him off to focus on the voice in her ear.

"Her communication piece is in full working order," replied Allura.

Alice felt *her* heart rate elevate. "Then what's going on?"

"Perhaps," said Allura, "she took it out."

"For what?" Alice demanded, but she didn't expect Allura, or anyone but Vel herself, to know.

She grunted, then turned to Dan. "Okay, I need you to give Don Won a lift, Dan. It'll be a long walk back to the ship. Think you can make it?"

"Yes, Captain!"

Caid stepped forward. "Alice, you look concerned. What story are you telling yourself about where Vel is?"

"None," she snapped. "She's probably on her way back to the ship, hasn't gotten there yet, and her comm fell out without her realizing it. Or someone's talking with her or she's ignoring me."

"Are you worried?"

"About Susy?" Alice laughed defiantly. "Are you kidding? She could literally disarm a person with a smile. She's not someone to worry about."

And yet ...

For all Vel's qualities that Alice found obnoxious or extra, the woman stuck to protocol. She wouldn't take off without notifying her captain.

Ah, that must be what happened, thought Alice. Vel *had* told her where she was going, but Alice hadn't heard (or hadn't been paying attention). "She'll meet us back at *Emergence,* I'm sure. Allura?"

"Yes, Daddy?"

"If Susy reaches out to you, tell her to head back in."

"Yes, Daddy."

Alice turned back to the group. "Okay, Pon, need a ride back to the committee?"

The Jejoon's watery, cowlike eyes glistened. "I don't know if my heart can take it! But yes!"

Once Pon Pon and Don Won had mounted their steeds, the group took off, stopping first at the committee to say goodbye to Pon and then onward toward *Emergence.*

But when they arrived inside the DeepCUT, Vel wasn't there.

The lieutenant was officially missing.

CHAPTER
NINETEEN

Don Won made himself comfortable on a chair at the back of the bridge, where Dan had set out a plate of warm rolls that looked a lot like the blob himself. As the Jejoon munched and prattled on about his boring life to an attentive Caid, Alice paced the length of the bridge and tried not to check the clock as it ticked down.

She did a piss-poor job of it. Eight hours left to complete the mission, and they still needed to convince the queen to sign off on this match in person and notify Liz Windsor of it.

And still, no sign of Vel.

Alice stopped her pacing and slumped into the captain's chair. "We're screwed." The Location forest was all she could see through the large window. Dark, deep, secretive.

She felt a gentle hand on her shoulder. "Captain," said Dan, "we don't have much more time to waste. You need to make a decision."

"Remind me of the options?"

"We wait for Vel and risk failing the mission, or we leave

without her to complete our mission then come back here for her once we've succeeded."

Alice dragged a hand down her face, groaning. "I suppose there aren't any dangers on Location she can't manage." She slapped the armrests of her captain's chair. "Seems cruel to leave her under the rule of the Committee of Boring People to Death, but I reckon this is what she would want us to do. Mission first." She got to her feet. "Okay, then, Dan. You've convinced me. Let's take off for—"

The window to the forest disappeared, replaced by an unfamiliar face. "Crew of DeepCUT *Emergence*. My name is Ankah Blum." The deep voice led Alice to believe it was a male face speaking to them, but not much else indicated gender to her. His skin was gray-brown like oak tree bark, but smooth like a mask. No lips, just a slit of a mouth, and three eyes, sea green, unblinking, as he—it—continued speaking. "I am a commander of the Alliance, and we have your captain."

Alice snorted. "What? Um, that's not possible because—"

Dan grabbed her arm and squeezed. Hard. Handling all those weapons had given him quite a grip.

Alice looked at him, but he didn't return the gaze. His eyes were fixed to the screen.

"You have Captain Machiavelli?" Dan said.

Ankah Blum replied, "Yes. We have her and we will not kill her if you meet us for negotiations. We have demands for the Depot we want you to deliver."

"I beg your pardon," Alice said, "but who the hell are you again?"

"We are the Alliance. We are everywhere and nowhere."

"Okay, but you're *somewhere*, because you want us to meet you."

"Yes, that is true."

Motion in her periphery caught her attention as Caid appeared at her side for moral support.

Alice had met this kind of bully before. Ankah Blum wasn't a born bully, that much was obvious. But he'd been bullied long enough that he knew how to mimic the behavior.

"I tell y'all what," Alice said, "we're more than likely to agree to them right off, because it's no skin off our backs what the Depot has to do to meet our end of the bargain. Let us know what you want right now, we'll agree to it, then you hand over our, uh, captain."

"We will only meet face to face."

Staring at the fifteen-foot visage of Ankah Blum seemed *extra* "face to face" to Alice. Her eyes jumped to the clock again. "Unfortunately, we don't have time for this, Mr. Blum. Can the rendezvous wait until, like, tomorrow?"

"Stop bluffing. We know you cannot complete your mission without your captain. Meet us at the designated spot now, or your captain dies."

Dan stepped forward. "How do we know she's not already dead?"

Ankah Blum motioned to someone off screen, and a moment later, Vel's face appeared. She was gagged and one of her eyes was swollen, but that didn't stop her from trying to yell insults at her captors.

It was clear that apprehending her had involved a fight, but no one on DeepService Team One would've expected any less. "Captain," Alice said, "hold tight. We're coming to get you."

Vel yelled something that sounded an awful lot like "own."

"We have sent the meeting coordinates to your ship,"

Ankah Blum said. "We will not stay here long, as the rest of the Depot now has access to those coordinates and will likely be coming to meet us in full force. Make a decision soon, Lieutenant Zone, or you, your crew aid, and Janitor Luck can say goodbye to your captain."

The screen dissolved into the surrounding forest again, and Alice blinked as reality set in. "Did he call me Janitor Luck?"

"Alice," said Caid, "I understand that must not feel great for your ego, but I think there are more important things to focus on right now."

"You're right." She glanced at the clock again. There was no way to make this work, was there? "Allura, can you reach Liz Windsor for me?"

When the liaison's face appeared on the screen, Alice felt a degree calmer. This was the obvious solution. Liz Windsor would understand, and she'd have their back. "Hi, Liz Windsor. I have a request to make. Could we get a smidgeon of an extension on the deadline for this mission? Just, like, ten hours?"

Liz Windsor smiled. "I figured you would ask for something like this, especially when I learned you had decided to match the Bacc'nalis to the Jejoons. What a stroke of inspired genius! I'm sure it will be a great match, but the Jejoons *are* known to be a slow-moving race."

Alice chuckled with relief. "You have no idea. So, ten extra hours is fine?"

"Oh. I'm sorry. No, no." Liz Windsor's smile erased itself. "There will be no extension. Strict protocol. Forty-eight hours should have been plenty of time. Normally, we only give our crews that much per assignment, unless special consideration is needed. If you can't do it in a forty-eight ship hours, I'm afraid you're not DeepService Team

One material. Best of fortune to you all! I know you can do it!"

The screen flickered off.

"Son of a bitch!" Alice turned to Dan and Caid, who stood silently behind her. "What do we do?"

The hologram tilted his head to the side. "This is an unfair situation for you to be in, Alice."

"No *shit*. Dan. What do we do?"

"I— I—I'm not the captain!"

"Well, neither am I, apparently!" She flopped back into her chair.

Seconds ticked off the clock.

"If we leave Susy, we still have a chance of completing the match, getting paid, and *not* getting banished. Then we can circle back and try to get her before the Alliance does anything crazy."

Dan wrung his hands. "I doubt the Alliance would allow that. If they don't kill her as soon as it's clear we're not going straight there, they could just as well disappear with her where we can never find them. Or Vel."

Alice wasn't willing to accept that she had no good options yet, though it was starting to look that way. "If we go after her, we probably won't complete the mission in time, we'll lose the money, be banished, but we might save Susy, who will also then be banished." She paused. "What would Susy do?"

Dan shook his head somberly. "I think she would tell us to complete the mission and leave her behind."

Alice scrunched her nose. "That doesn't feel right, though, does it?"

"I love that you're tuning into your feelings," Caid said.

"Not at all," said Dan. "Doesn't feel right at all."

"Allura, can the escape pods jump a time fold?" she asked.

"No, Daddy. They lack the technical capabilities to do that on their own."

"Damn. So that means we can't send one of us to take Don Won to Bacc'nalia." There had to be some way. There *had* to be. "Allura, if we met the Alliance at the location they've provided, could we theoretically have enough time to go there, get Susy, then travel to Bacc'nalia to introduce Don Won to Queen Phet?"

And then Allura spoke the sexiest words Alice had ever heard: "Yes, Daddy."

"And how much time would that give us on Bacc'nalia?"

"The time remaining minus travel time would leave you forty-eight minutes and forty-two seconds to meet and bargain with the Alliance, return to the ship, and then meet with Queen Phet to have her sign the papers."

"So you're telling me there's a chance," Alice muttered. She slapped her thighs and stood to face her crew. "Right. This is going to be a fucking doozy. Y'all ready? We're gonna go get Susy back."

CHAPTER
TWENTY

By the time they found the meeting place on the planet Peeorg VFP3787, the plan was in place. Don Won was precious cargo and absolutely useless in a fight, so he would remain on *Emergence* under the watchful eye of Caid, who was also fairly useless in a fight. While the hologram wouldn't be able to physically stop Don Won from doing as he pleased, it went unspoken that the therapist could probably talk the little blob out of whatever ill-advised plans he might make. And if that didn't work, Caid could break him down emotionally until his legs stopped working.

That meant it was up to Alice and Dan to get this rescue mission knocked out as quickly as possible.

"I've never felt so hot," Alice said, standing beside her crewmate in the hangar, sporting her turquoise jumpsuit and with weapons strapped to every available inch of her. To obscure the firepower they each were packing, they'd also donned long fur coats that were usually only reserved for the coldest of planetary climates.

"Yes," Dan said, adjusting his shoulders under his coat.

"My body temperature is unpleasant. Thankfully, Peeorg VFP3787 is relatively cold."

"That's not what I mean. I'm talking about how I could end an entire civilization right now by sneezing at the wrong time. By the way, what's with the planetary names? Peeorg VFP3787?"

"Peeorg is the name of the person who first added the planet to the intergalactic catalogue."

"You're telling me a guy named Blerg added my home planet?"

"Indeed."

"And the VFP?"

"It's a classification that takes into account climate, atmosphere, and threat level. VFP indicates that it is a Very Fine Planet."

"Oh! Sweet! That's probably the nicest thing anyone's ever said about Earth. What about the other one, the one for Location?"

"JFP. It was a Just Fine Planet. A category below VFP."

"And then the numbers at the end indicate just how many planets of that type the person has found?"

"Correct! You're getting the hang of this space thing, Captain."

"With your help, Dan." She placed a hand on his shoulder. "This is going to be dangerous as all get out. The odds are sure as hell against us. I can't imagine us making it through this without at least one onset of the jitters. You prepared for that?"

Dan reached into his coat pocket and pulled out four boosters. "I am."

"Jesus H.! How'd you get four? Can *I* get four?"

"I saved up mine and told Allura I needed Vel's allotment for the day in case we found her."

"We will. And come to think of it, she looked like shit salad on the screen. A booster might be exactly what she needs."

Dan squinted at her. "Vel has been held captive and is furious from having been overpowered. You really think she'll need a booster to get her through this?"

Alice wagged a finger at him. "Fair point. As soon as we get that psycho untied, she'll be a booster."

The ship jolted. Touch down. "Okay, Dan. We got this. And if we don't …" She held up her favorite blaster.

Dan toasted her with a booster packet. "Lead the way, Captain."

Allura's voice crooned directions in Alice's ear from the moment they set foot on Peeorg VFP3787. Whether it was, in fact, a Very Fine Planet was something Alice didn't have a spare thought for. It was a planet. It reminded her vaguely of Sedona, Arizona, a place she'd visited one spring break with a sort-of boyfriend who claimed he was a psychic medium.

She could breathe on this planet, and she could also run on it, so that was what she and Dan did. They made it into a marketplace, and the smell of cooking meat hit her senses. The streets were full of creatures of all shapes and sizes whom Alice would've very much liked to gawk at in other circumstances. But not now; there was no time. "Hard left. So hard," Allura instructed them.

They took a left after a fruit vendor's tent, and as Alice rounded the corner, she ran into something solid and realized it was a misplaced tree trunk.

Wait. No…

A foot. A giant fucking foot.

She looked up to see what it was attached to and got an eyeful of alien genitals. "Blerk!" She sidestepped and hurried after Dan, who'd continued ahead of her. "Are we on schedule, Allura?"

"A full minute ahead, Daddy."

"Perfect."

"Left at the fork."

Alice caught up to Dan, who had also received the directions in his earpiece and didn't need to be told to veer left.

They arrived at the door of the arranged meeting spot. It was in an empty alley, set into the stone exterior of a building that stretched the length of the block and reached up an easy fifty feet.

"What now?" Dan asked. "Do we knock?"

"Let's see." Alice stepped forward and banged on the door. Her heart was racing, and while she was glad for a break to catch her breath, her impatience kicked in almost immediately while they waited for someone to respond to the knocking.

"Knock again," Dan said.

"Why don't you?" she snapped. "I'm just the janitor."

Dan rolled his eyes, but before his knock could make contact, the door swung open.

A hunchbacked figure stood in the threshold, eyeing the arrivals through suspicious slits that could've been gills. The thing wore a pile of clothing that was as gray as it was brown, and from beneath this animate laundry hamper came a gruff, androgynous voice. "D'you 'ave an appointment?"

"Oh, uh, I'm sorry," said Alice. This was not what she had expected at all. Her functioning assumption had been that she would not only be expected but recognized. "Are you— Are you with the Alliance?"

The laundry hamper snorted something phlegmy. "No."

"Okay. Then I guess we got the wrong place."

"You're in the right spot," Allura whispered before adding, "Daddy."

"D'you 'ave an appointment with the Alliance, then?" asked the laundry hamper.

"Yes. It's sort of a big deal. They have our captain."

"Ahh." The hunchback leaned forward. "An 'ostage negotiation. Yeah, I think I saw one o' those on the schedule today. What was your name, love?"

"Um. Alice Luck and Dan Zone?" She looked to Dan for answers, but he appeared as lost as she was.

"Well, you two might as well come in while I look it up on the books."

The hunchback motioned for them inside, and though this *couldn't* be right—it lacked some of the trademarks of a hostage negotiation Alice had considered vital, chief among them a shared sense of urgency—she motioned for Dan to go ahead of her and then followed.

The room they entered had electric lighting, but what it didn't have was a reliable current, and the bulbs flickered overhead as the laundry hamper led them into an austere waiting area with only one long stone bench and a small desk. The hunchback huddled behind the desk, though *most* of what it did would be classified as "huddling," so there was nothing remarkable about that.

A large book was already open on the desk, and the hamper ran a bony finger over the lines until... "Ah, Janitor Alice Luck and Lieutenant Dan Zone. Yes, here we are. It looks like you are scheduled to be meeting with Alliance—

forgive me, that's all it says, 'Alliance'—one minute from now in ransom room eight."

"You're not with the Alliance, then?" Dan asked the laundry hamper.

"I already told ye that."

"Then who are you?"

"Bagknock. Least, that's wha' they call me. Not sure why."

"And this place? What is it?"

"Ah, well, we 'andle all your terroristic logistics, don't we? Not everyone 'as an 'ideout for an 'ostage right when they need one, do they? So, they subcontract with us. Our cells are the best in this arm of the spiral, and we even offer in-'ouse services to keep the prisoners alive yet emaciated. Captors like 'em better that way. 'Ard to convince the other side their loved one's in danger if they got a round belly an' a glow about 'em, eh? There's an art to keeping an 'ostage in the right condition, and we know 'ow it's done!"

Alice stepped between Dan and Bagknock. "This is very interesting, but we're in a bit of a time crunch. Can we ..." She waved to get on with it.

"Well, well, well," Bagknock said. "You'll not likely come out on the better end of a negotiation with a sense of urgency like that, sugarplum. They'll know they got leverage on ya, won't they?"

Alice pressed her hands together in prayer. "Please take us to room eight. Please."

"You'll be doing the talking, won't ya?" Bagknock said to Dan.

"Of course."

And as the hamper led the way down the long, dark hall, cells of hostages on their right, pay-per-hour ransom rooms on their left, Dan continued to question Bagknock about the business structure.

"So you're the receptionist of this thing?"

Bagknock made an unfriendly gurgling sound. "You assume I'm the receptionist, eh? You saying that because you think I'm a female?"

Dan gasped. "Oh, no! Of course not. I know men can be receptionists, too."

"*Men?*" The hamper spoke the word as if it tasted of rusty metal. "What business does a man 'ave being a receptionist? No way. Not one of those, I'm not."

Alice lagged a few steps behind. "Allura," she whispered. "How are we on time?"

"One minute behind schedule, Daddy."

"'Ere we are," Bagknock said. "Ransom room eight." It paused and turned to inspect the two clients. "I like ye. I 'ope ye get what ye came 'ere for. 'Oomever that is. I 'ave 'alf a mind to give ye some pointers before I let ye inside."

"Thank you, Bagknock, but you've already done plenty," said Dan. "You've answered my questions, and that was more than you needed to do. I appreciate it."

Bagknock hunched even further. "Ye could do a better job concealing those weapons, ye could."

"Right." Dan bowed his gratitude then adjusted his furs, which had been displaced in the scramble.

Alice did the same, and before Bagknock opened the door, she shared a last look with Dan. This was it. They were going in to try to get their crewmate back. And time was not on their side.

"In and out," Alice whispered.

"Mmm ..." came a voice in her ear.

"Subservience mode, Allura."

The door opened, and Alice and Dan stepped forward

into the most hostile environment she had ever faced, including that one parent-teacher meeting after she'd been caught snorting crushed sour candies behind the middle school gym.

"Lieutenant Zone. We were wondering if you would show. And you brought ... the ship janitor." The woman who spoke arched a bushy eyebrow as she took Alice in from head to toe.

In all, five members of the Alliance were waiting for them in the room, and almost all of them looked humanoid. One, however, looked like a cactus, thorns and all, but the others each had two legs, two arms, a torso, eyes, a nose, and a mouth. Alice was beginning to realize such a checklist was about all she should hope for in outer space. It still allowed for vast physical variation, but when there weren't extra or missing limbs to mentally contend with, it made the adjustment easier for her human brain to handle.

She decided to ignore the cactus, or rather, treat it as if it were a cactus, even though it had a large blaster slung over one of its arms.

No reason to get freaked out by a gun and a cactus, she assured herself. *If anything, it should make you feel at home.*

"Never underestimate the ship's janitor," Dan said, and Alice wished he could have said literally anything cooler on her behalf. But if they were to maintain the advantage of being underestimated, she would have to pretend to be a janitor for a little while longer. A janitor with a megablaster —booyah!

There was nothing wrong with being a janitor, of course. She'd befriended nearly every janitor at her high school, and not one of them gave her the impression that their criminal background check was as squeaky clean as they left the gymnasium floors. They also knew who had the best weed from having smelled it around campus and pointed her in the right direction a few times. It was a known fact that anyone who could clean the boys' bathroom day in and day out without up and quitting wasn't someone to be trifled with.

But even taking all that into consideration, she didn't love being called a janitor when she was the goddamn *captain.*

"I am Astra Blum," said the woman. "These are my associates whose names are not of consequence to you. Please, have a seat."

"We're in a bit of a hurry," Alice said.

The leader, whose face was the color of moonlight, frowned. "What, the toilets won't clean themselves?"

"Ignore her," Dan said. "She's from Earth."

That seemed to speak volumes to the Alliance members. Volumes Alice had never read, had never even heard the titles of.

"She's not incorrect, though," Dan continued. "We're pressed for time. We have a lot at stake. If we don't complete our mission in the allotted time, which is quickly dwindling, we will lose our pay. And the Depot will banish us."

"Then it looks like we share a common adversary."

In the end, all parties remained standing, the table merely functioning as a physical divider of the two sides.

"The Depot is our employer, not our adversary," Dan explained. "What harm have they done to you?"

"What harm?" Astra chuckled dryly. "Do you not know for whom you work? The Depot is the adversary of all *but* the Depot."

"As I said, they are not our adversary."

"Then you are the Depot."

"No," Dan replied. "We only work for them."

"You don't yet see. No one can have a relationship with the Depot. You will be swallowed by them too, one day. Maybe not far off."

"You're right," Alice said. "Not far off at all. Especially if we don't hurry this up. Where's Captain Machiavelli?"

Astra glared at the feisty janitor. "She's being held in a secure cell until we can reach an arrangement."

"How can you expect us to discuss any arrangement," Alice said, "when we don't even know you haven't killed her since the last time we spoke?"

Astra looked Alice up and down. "You're awfully mouthy for a shit sweeper. You must be excellent at toilets to have gotten the job."

"Stop avoiding the question," Dan said. "How can we know our captain is safe?"

Astra frowned then turned to one of her cronies. "Bring her in."

Alice tried to not let it show that this was the first step of an especially harebrained plan.

Two cronies left (not the cactus, unfortunately) and returned a moment later with Vel. Each had a tight grip of her under the armpit, though her hands were tied behind her back and her ankles were hobbled. Her mouth was gagged, too, but they really should've put a bag over her head, because the deadliest feature on her face at the moment wasn't her mouth, but her murderous eyes.

Vel tried to speak through the gag, but her words were, of course, muffled to shit.

"Looks like we made a smart move muzzling her," a man next to Astra said. "She's still trying to bark orders to her crew."

In reality, Vel was doing no such thing. She was trying to

say something very different, which Alice and Dan wouldn't find out for a few more minutes.

"Now that you can see she's alive," Astra said, "let's talk."

Dan clenched his fists. "Lay out your demands."

"We want you to spy on the Depot for us. We need to know their next move so that we can counter it and possibly appeal to the ICC."

"What's the ICC got to do with this?" Dan asked.

"What's the ICC?" Alice asked.

"The Intergalactic Commerce Court. They handle—"

"Commerce. Yeah. Got it."

Dan turned back to the Alliance. "Why are you so anti-Depot? What have they ever done to you?"

Astra guffawed. "Are you kidding? They've stolen our livelihoods! Lilqua'tartian here"—she inclined her head toward her cactus crony—"used to run the most prosperous transit business in his solar system. Made a good living—was able to employ many of his people so that they could earn a good living, too, running transits between planets. He had his fair share of close competitors, sure, but that made for good business, and they all were able to throw back a strong drink together at the MultiInterTransit awards. But then," Astra said, lowering her voice, "the Depot expanded its transportation services into Lilqua'tartian's solar system. They undercut his viable prices by half until he couldn't hold on any longer. Not only did his business go under, but so did all of his local competitors."

"But what about the consumer?" Dan asked defiantly. "What about the consumer who won in the end with the lower prices?"

"Ha! You think that the Depot kept the prices low once

its competition had been crushed? No way. Tell them, Lilqua'tartian."

To Alice's surprise, the cactus rocked forward a pace. "The price of a journey from Moppa to Grogolama is *twice* what it was when I was in business!" His voice was gravelly and chock-full of resentment.

Dan gasped. "So not even the *consumer* is coming out on top?"

"I'm sorry," Alice said. "This is *really* boring, and we're shaving it *very* close. Can we get back to the hostage negotiation?"

"We've made our demand," Astra said. "You spy for us. Oh, and you pay us half of your earnings to fund our start-ups."

"*What?*" Alice spat. "Get fucked."

"Fine," Astra said, "assuming your lieutenant agrees with your approach, you're welcome to walk away right now. No harm will come to either of you, and you can complete your mission. Once you all end up dead and another crew is brought in to replace you, we'll simply offer them the same bargain. We'll get what we want one way or another."

"Hold up," Alice said. "*You* were the ones who tried to kill us, weren't you? You tried to assassinate us on Bacc'nalia!"

But as soon as she'd spoken, she could tell from the slight angling of Astra's head that the woman had no knowledge of that. "Why would we try to kill you *before* negotiating?"

"That's a good question," Dan said. "I don't think you would."

Astra looked to the rest of her crew, who shook their heads. "*We* didn't do anything of that sort."

"Then who was it?" Dan asked. "Do you know?"

"Could have been anyone."

"If you had to guess, though?"

Astra looked hesitant, but then said, "There are many factions of the Alliance. Not all agree on the best approach to getting what we want."

"But you do believe it was another faction of the Alliance?"

"It's possible. The Mautir Complex faction has been known to employ what some might refer to as unnecessarily dramatic tactics."

"I believe you," Dan said. "You have to know we can't spy for you, and we can't leave our captain behind. You've put us in an impossible position, no matter how sympathetic we might be to your situation."

"Of course you can spy for us," Astra said. "You don't *want* to."

"No," Dan said, "we literally cannot." He tapped his earpiece. "Everything about our trip and this conversation is being logged. We cannot become your spies because the Depot now knows about your offer."

The option of turning around and leaving was looking more and more appealing, Alice thought. But then she made a grave tactical error. She looked at Vel.

The fire in Vel's eyes had burned down to embers. Creases around her eyes spoke of a tired resignation, to pain, to death, to abandonment by her captain.

Getting Susy out of there would be a mess. It might end up with all of them being killed, or worse, being taken captive and held indefinitely while the Alliance tried to bargain with the Depot for their lives. Alice didn't know much about her employer, but what she did know led her to believe there was no bargain to be struck with them.

Dan was right; spying would be impossible. Meeting the Alliance's demands was out of the question.

With time ticking down in Alice's chest, it was clear any attempt at saving Vel would probably end poorly. They could leave now and still make it to Queen Phet on time. She could split. Take off. Maybe drink for a while until she felt less guilty. Maybe hang out on Bacc'nalia and party away the shame of leaving one of her crew behind.

Or.

For once in her life, she could stick it out. She wouldn't run away and distract herself. She wouldn't hop on the first spaceship that came by offering her an escape from a rooftop proposal.

Vel would do the same for her, she was certain of it.

"Dan," she whispered, "you still got those boosters?"

He turned his head slowly toward her, his eyes two black and endless eddies. "Alice. No."

"Slam 'em back, my friend."

"No," he whimpered.

Alice didn't look away from Dan's fearful face. "Slam. Them."

As Astra demanded to know what the hell was going on, Alice saw something switch on in Dan's eyes.

Oh, hell yeah, she thought.

He tossed all four booster tablets into his mouth as Vel looked on in horror and then excitement from her position in the corner of the room.

"Stop him!" Astra said, and her remaining cronies who were neither holding Vel nor a cactus scrambled around the table barrier to try to knock the boosters out of his mouth. Too late.

Alice threw her furs off, shouting, "Stay where you are." She went for the biggest blaster she had first, because why not? If she was gonna do it, she was gonna do it in style.

"Untie her," Dan demanded.

"We don't have to listen to you," Astra spat. "You think we didn't know you would come armed?"

Alice wasn't sure when it had happened, but next thing she knew, Lilqua'tartian had the barrel of a blaster leveled at her head.

Could she get a shot off before the cactus fired? How quick were cactus reflexes?

Astra didn't bother to draw a weapon. She didn't need to. There were already blasters aimed at each of the DeepService Team One members.

"It's a Mexican standoff," Alice breathed, her heart racing. "I've always wanted to be in one of these."

"You have?" Dan asked, his blaster pointed at the man whose blaster was pointed at Vel's head.

"Well, I thought I did. But now that I'm looking at it, it presents a problem, doesn't it?"

A sudden knock on the meeting room door so nearly made someone in the room pull their trigger and initiate a mass slaughter that a sensual shiver ran through Dan's body.

"'Ey, we got another one from the crew," came Bagknock's craggy voice. "Says 'e 'as something to say to ye."

Dan and Alice remained silent, holding their breath until Astra said, "Fine, send him in."

The blaster barrels remained locked on their targets as the door opened and Caid Sonorian stepped in. He appeared in a jumpsuit and furs, like the others, and if Alice didn't already know he was a hologram, she wouldn't have guessed. He looked very *massy*.

"Hi, I'm sorry to interrupt." When Astra drew her weapon on him, he didn't react, and why would he? "I wanted to come in and see if I could help speed things up and reach a resolution where everyone would come away feeling like they had their needs both heard and met."

"Nice try," Astra said. "This has gone beyond anyone being *heard*."

Caid inched away from the rest of DeepService Team One until he stood alone on the opposite side of the room from where Vel was held.

Why was he doing that? Alice wondered. Something about this was way off. Caid, as a rule, moved *closer* to people every chance he could, not farther away.

And then it hit her. Holy infertile cow. Of course! They didn't know he was a hologram. And he knew they didn't know. Was he really about to …?

"Gosh, I hear that," Caid continued. "I can tell you're feeling hurt and wronged. It's okay to admit someone violated you." He then addressed one of the men with his blaster pointed at Vel's head. "And you. I can see the hurt in your eyes. But I can also see the strength. I admire that you've been able to pick yourself up and rebuild with this group of people. I bet you feel closer to them because of your shared cause than you've felt toward most people, huh? You don't want anyone to start firing! Of course you don't! None of us do. We all have people we care about in this room. Let's take a breath before we do anything that can't be undone."

Alice snuck a glance at Dan, whose right eye was twitching violently, which she assumed had less to do with the quantum jitters and more to do with tossing back four boosters at once. He grinned like a fool, which only helped to confuse the situation.

The man with the blaster on Vel began to falter. Caid was breaking through. The barrel dropped toward the floor, and slowly, the man met Caid's eyes.

"There you go," said the therapist. "You wouldn't hurt a bound and gagged prisoner. That's not you. If you were to shoot someone, it would be someone pointing a blaster at you, and that's totally understandable. That's part of a natural survival instinct. You aren't the type to kill brutally, only in self-defense."

What in the actual hell was going on? Caid's voice had fallen into a rhythm that left Alice feeling like she was floating. Would this frustratingly sexy idiot pull it off and defuse this situation?

It might happen.

And then it didn't.

Caid shouted, "You'll always be a disappointment to your father!" as he threw off his fur and produced the biggest blaster Alice had ever seen, aiming it right at the man next to Vel.

The violent response was immediate, and every last bit of it was directed at the hologram.

They didn't have long. Dan leaped toward Vel, curling as he flew through the air. He became an armored bowling ball that sustained no damage as one of the guards shifted his fire away from Caid and toward the pearly object hurtling toward him.

Dan took out one of Vel's captors at the knees, and while the other was distracted, Alice kicked him in the face, took his spot, and scanned the room for anyone who might look this way instead of continuing to fire at Caid. None of the Alliance seemed to realize he hadn't fired back yet. Caid put on quite the act, jerking around and howling, pretending the bullets and lasers weren't sailing right through him, though anyone paying close attention would realize the wall behind him was taking the brunt of the damage.

Dan unfurled and already had a knife in his hands, cutting the binds on Vel's hands. She ripped the gag out of her mouth. "You idiots! You should have left me."

"Don't make us regret it," Alice said, struggling to be heard above the weapon blasts.

"I don't think I'll have to."

"The key," Dan said. "I don't have the key to the hobbles."

Vel's eyes jumped to the cactus. "That one. He's got them."

Unfortunately, Lilqua'tartian was out of reach. "Where?" Dan shouted.

"I dunno, a pouch? I think he has a pouch under one of those spiky arms."

Without another word, Dan threw himself toward the cactus, balling up in midair and opening his protective sphere long enough to reach an arm out and stick it inside the cactus.

But Lilqua'tartian felt the pressure, and whipped his weapon around toward Dan.

BOOM.

The recoil knocked Alice back a step as her shot took the arm right off the cactus.

Dan snagged the keys and tossed them through the air. Vel caught them easily and had the hobbles off in an instant.

"Forget him!" Astra shouted. "He's a hologram, you idiots!" She had her blaster out now, having drawn it on Caid, but when she turned it toward the others, it was already too late.

Dan had been right—Vel needed no boosters. She *was* one.

She kicked the blaster from Astra's grasp, grabbed the woman's head between her hands, and then head-butted it out. Astra crumpled to the floor.

She took after the guards next, taking one down with a kick in the groin, another by a chop to the neck. "Go," she said, her voice seemingly unaffected by the frenzy of violence.

Rather than reminding Vel who the actual captain was, Alice did as she was told.

Flinging open the ransom room door, she chanced a look behind her. Dan sprinted past her and out into the hallway, and Caid followed behind, clearly trying to fit with the mood of urgency despite having none himself.

As Alice waited for Vel to wrap things up, one of the Alliance goons recovered and got a shot off that missed Alice's nose by a few inches, ricocheted off the edge of the door, and missed her ear by even less.

She let out a low whistle. "Susy, let's go!"

The warrior's focus broke for a second when she turned and saw Alice waiting for her. She blinked. And in that micro moment, a recovered crony aimed his sights on her.

Alice didn't think, and for once, that was the correct way to respond. She sprinted, full bore, conjured up the tackling practice her oldest brother had given her over the years, leveled her shoulders, and ran right through the shooter.

She could feel the heat of the blaster shot in her hair and hoped to God it hadn't caught her on fire.

Strong hands grabbed the back of her jumpsuit and lifted her off the groaning heap. She turned around, ready to throw a punch but it was, of course, only Vel.

"Good form. Let's go."

The two women sprinted out of the room, down the hallway, and past Bagknock, who was still shouting after

Dan and Caid that someone better pay the rest of the reservation fee or there would be trouble.

They hauled ass back to *Emergence* without speaking a word, weaving through the streets, shoving people aside as needed.

Only once they were back into the sunshine did Alice realize how profusely blood was pouring from Vel's side.

CHAPTER
TWENTY-ONE

"Go!" Alice shouted the second they were back on *Emergence.* "Get us the hell out of here and back to Bacc'nalia."

"Yes, Daddy."

Alice braced herself on her knees to catch her breath in the hangar. She hadn't bothered to grab her coat on the way out, and counted it as no real loss, especially since she'd returned with all the blasters she'd left with. That was what mattered.

Dan and Caid had beaten them back, but not by much. Had Alice ever run so fast in her life? She was built for wrestling, not sprinting. But what she wasn't going to do was let the injured lieutenant whoop her ass in a head-to-head. Hell no.

She paid for it in screaming muscles and aching lungs.

"Vel!" Dan exclaimed, rushing over. "What happened?"

Vel pressed her hands to her side where the blood continued to seep. "The void-headed goon got a shot off at the last second."

"Let me see it."

Vel cringed and slowly removed her hands.

Dan looked at it from a few angles, the overhead lights of the hangar deck glistening on his armor. "Okay, we gotta get you cleaned up before I can see what we're working with. Far too much blood."

Alice clasped her fingers together above her head. "How did you … run so … fast?"

"It's not a terrible injury," Vel said. "I've had worse. That jerk would've gotten me right through the middle if you hadn't tackled him."

"Mmm …" Caid said mournfully, pressing a hand to his heart. "That was so much trauma for everyone, wasn't it? The experience will be settling in your psyche for the next few days, and you may experience some moments of emotional volatility as that happens."

Alice held up a hand. "Caid, thank you for what you did back there—it was genius and worked like a charm—but can you please shut the hell up for, like, fifteen or twenty minutes?"

Since Vel was able to walk, they let her shower without assistance, though Dan waited anxiously outside her cabin door for the go-ahead to enter and properly tend to her wounds.

As it turned out, the blast had grazed Vel below the ribs, and Allura confirmed through MRI imaging that the damage was only superficial. This was the first anyone had heard about Allura's MRI capabilities, and no one felt totally okay about her looking inside them whenever she wished. But they let it slide.

Vel refused to stay in bed, so now all five of them—Dan, Vel, Alice, Caid, and Don Won—sat on the bridge, waiting out the rest of the trip via time fold back to Bacc'nalia.

It would feel like only a few hours, but Alice was

learning that her feelings didn't matter so much to space-time.

"Allura?"

"Yes, Daddy?"

"I'm afraid to even ask, but how are we on time?"

"Eight minutes behind schedule. Upon landing, you'll have seventeen minutes to get Queen Phet to sign the agreement and to notify the Depot that the mission is complete."

Vel groaned but was merciful enough—or perhaps tired enough, since Dan had consumed her boosters for the day—to refrain from reiterating that they shouldn't have wasted time rescuing her.

Alice turned to Don Won, who was playing chess with Caid at the dining table in the back of the bridge. "Sorry, buckaroo, but if the queen wants to take you for a test drive, it's gonna have to be a quicky."

Dan perked up from where he was reclining in a heated massage chair. His armor, while not penetrated, had taken quite a beating. "You can't hurry the process with the Bacc'nalis, Captain. Very rude. Queen Phet won't like it at all."

"You kidding me?" Alice said. "You think Don Won here *isn't* a two-pump chump? It would be hard to make it last *more* than a couple of minutes the first time."

"Captain Luck," Dan said, his tone growing grave. "I know we're under a time crunch, but—"

"Give it a rest." It was Vel who spoke. "I'd rather be rude than dead, wouldn't you?"

Dan Zone from the Department of Weapons and Culture considered it, then leaned back in his heated chair. "As we say, when culture fails, there's always weapons."

CHAPTER
TWENTY-TWO

"I'm afraid of heights!" Don Won moaned.

"Hell of a time to mention it," Alice said, as the roof of Queen Phet's castle rose to meet them.

Rappelling from *Emergence* onto the palace hadn't been part of the original plan, but since they were still four minutes behind, corners had to be cut.

Once the queen had promised not to shoot at the ship when it entered airspace above her home, the plan was set, and Dan walked them through using the onboard equipment.

As Alice quickly found out, beaming people up and down was not a real thing. Physics "couldn't work that way." What a fucking disappointment.

Emergence hovered steady above them, but winds had picked up, and even Vel was beginning to look a little green in the gills as she swayed on her cable.

Caid, of course, was having no problems with the descent.

They touched down, and Alice moaned as she felt her feet hit the solid ground of the roof. Not time to sigh relief yet. For one, the time, but for another, Bacc'nali architecture was still shit, and if she didn't watch her step, she might find herself falling through multiple stories of this place *without* a harness.

"Okay, you little sex marshmallow," she said, turning to Don Won. "Let's get you laid."

Alice grabbed him by the hand and dragged him after her to the roof access door. From there, Allura provided directions the rest of the way to the queen's chambers.

"How we doing on time?" Alice asked.

"Rappelling gave you six minutes back. You're now only two minutes behind."

When the group reached the antechamber to the queen's quarters, Alice was shocked to find Queen Phet nowhere, despite the arrangements they'd made only an hour before in ship time.

"We need to talk with the queen," Alice told one of the two guards standing outside the chamber door. "We're on her schedule, and it's urgent."

The guard who responded remained stock-still except for his mouth. "The queen has ordered us not to disturb her orgy."

"Orgy!" Alice exclaimed. "But ..." She looked at Don Won, who didn't seem to know what the word meant. "Come on, we need to talk to her. Like, *now*. We're sort of on a time crunch here."

But neither guard would be moved.

"Luck," Vel whispered from beside her. "Time."

"I know!" Alice replied. "Look, I understand your situation," she said to the guards, balling her hands into fists. "You won't want to anger Queen Phet. But I cannot stress enough how much we need to talk to her. Our futures rest on it."

The same guard who had spoken before replied, "No."

Alice heard Caid over her shoulder whisper, "Deep breaths. We'll find a way. I believe in you."

Oh, she'd find a way. She didn't need Caid to tell her that. It might not be a pretty way, and may turn into a shitshow, but she'd figure something out.

She always did.

The way she saw it, if she didn't do anything, or if the guards continued to not be moved, everyone on her crew was done-zo. Rest of their lives in Nowheresville.

But Alice was nothing if not an optimist at heart. With the stakes so high, almost every possible outcome would be better than the consequence of *not* finishing this mission.

She braced herself. "Peter Piper picked a peck of pickled peppers. If Peter Piper picked—"

The guards were shocked stupid for only a moment before they launched forward to defend their queen's honor.

"Wait!" Dan lunged forward, his hands up. "Your queen has given her blessing for Alice Luck to use that sound. If you kill her, your queen will kill you, too."

And now the guards were officially perplexed, though they wouldn't have used that word for obvious reasons.

The guards locked eyes, then the previously silent one said, "We should check, just in case."

And so it was that forty-six seconds later, Queen Phet threw open the doors to her bedroom and sauntered out naked into the antechamber. "Oh, is it that time already? I thought we were meeting tomorrow."

"Nope. Today, Your Majesty. May I introduce to you your proposed match: Don Won the Jejoon from Waff JFP990, better known as Location." Alice stepped to the side to reveal the queen's potential mate and held her breath.

The queen took him in, circling him slowly. Far too slowly.

"Why is he clothed?" she asked.

"Modesty is their custom," Alice said.

"Will he need to remain clothed while we engage?"

Alice deferred to Dan with a look.

"No, Your Majesty," he said. "It is customary for his folk to be nude during sexual engagement."

"He has all the right parts?"

Alice struggled against her impatience. "Yes. I made sure. All the genetics fit as well. I see no reason why he would not be able to impregnate you. His people and yours are a perfect match."

Except for the serious risk of mutations, she thought with an internal cringe.

A sly smile crept over Queen Phet's lips. "Very well. It will be an interesting challenge to mate with a new species."

"Begging Your Majesty," said Don Won, "don't hurt me."

"Oh, he *is* adorable! Yes, I'll definitely take him, and swiftly."

Caid leaned over to his new pal. "Do you consent, Don Won? I know it seems like a lot is on your shoulders, but the *last* thing we want is to be complicit in your traumatic sexual encounter."

"Uh, excuse me," Alice said, trying to waft the hologram out of her way with a few flicks of her wrists, "speak for yourself. The last thing *I* want is to fail this mission. If my guy mochi here has to take one for the team, well, who *hasn't*?"

Caid frowned. "This sounds like something we may need to unpack later."

Alice would not be doing that. She turned to the queen. "Okay, we're all set, right? Two tickets to Grindtown?"

The queen frowned. "I was thinking about a nap and a soak first. Fresh off a big orgy, and things got *active*."

Alice's stomach dropped into her feet. "You're *not in the mood?*" She shared an incredulous look with Dan, who shook his head, himself at a loss. In none of their plans had they anticipated that the Queen of Horndoggery might not feel like screwing when they arrived.

This was bad.

Vel's expression made it clear, though, that Phet and Don Won were going to bone if she had to smash them together herself. Alice didn't want it to come to that.

We're so close, she thought. And then that thought reminded her of an asset she could tap for this problem.

"Allura," she said.

"Yes, Daddy?"

"We need your help."

"I've never done anything like this before," Queen Phet said excitedly as she lounged on her gigantic four-poster bed. Don Won was at her side, looking terribly uncomfortable, though not uninterested, mumbling little self-assurances in barely audible tones.

"Okay," Alice said, standing beside the bed and wishing she could be anywhere else in the universe, doing anything else in existence. "Allura, feed me the lines." She swallowed hard and listened. And then, as the ship's operating system did what it did best, Alice began repeating the prompts aloud. "Don Won has never done anything like this before, and he's scared. Will you be gentle with him, or will you ... take him roughly?"

And so the dirty talk began as the seconds ticked down on the mission …

———

Vel and Dan shared an anxious look as they waited with Caid in the silent hall outside Queen Phet's bedroom. The bones set into the clay wall didn't help ease their nerves, and when Dan cleared his throat, the sound of it echoed menacingly down the dark, slick stone of the long corridor, leaving him feeling exposed.

Alice and Don Won were still in the queen's chambers, and though neither Vel nor Dan had any desire to imagine what was taking place behind those closed doors, as the minutes stretched on, their anxious curiosity got the best of them.

"You think she was forced to get in on the action?" Dan whispered.

"You think they'd have to force her?" Vel replied.

"I almost wish I could witness this beautiful connection of souls myself," Caid said. "Think about it. Separated by galaxies, brought together by fate. There could be the start of a whole new race of beings taking place behind those doors, and we're present for its conception."

Dan turned to the therapist. "Nothing is physically stopping you from going in there, right? I bet they wouldn't mind."

Caid was about to begin a speech on consent, but before he could, one of the double doors cracked open, and Alice slipped through. No, not slipped so much as stumbled. She blinked, swayed, and then staggered toward her crewmates.

"I've seen things. I didn't want to see them, but I have."

"Sh-sh-shh," Dan said, reaching out and pulling his

captain against his lumpy side for comfort.

"You're saying they're sexually engaging?" Vel asked.

Alice had to think about it. "Yes, I guess that's what it is. But what it *looked* like—" She tried to swallow, but her mouth was too dry.

"Was it beautiful?" Caid asked.

Alice shook her head adamantly. "Have you ever seen a dog hump a beanbag chair? I mean, really get after it? I had this roommate my sophomore year—"

"I don't think we need a story about this one," Vel said, folding her arms. "Are they done yet?"

"I don't know. It took a while to build the queen up to it, so they started. Whether this will be quick or take long is anyone's guess."

"It's *our* guess," Dan said. "It's our rumps on the line!"

"Allura," Alice rasped, "how much time do we have left?"

"Six minutes, Daddy."

Alice glanced nervously to her lieutenant. "And you have the—"

Vel whipped the electronic signature pad up from beneath her armpit. "Of course I do."

"Good, good." Alice had forgotten all about it in their preparation for rappelling from the ship. Whoops.

And so they waited, not patiently or with any professionalism.

Dan checked his watch obsessively. Alice paced, hugged herself, and chewed her nails. Vel grew steadily more spring-loaded for action, her breathing slowing down like the sea receding before a tsunami. Caid hummed and kept his eyes closed as he remained in a crane pose, his right foot against his left knee, his palms pressed together in front of him.

With three and a half minutes left, Alice sidled up to Dan. "Hey, theoretically, if we were to, oh, I dunno, go on the lam for a while until things blow over with the Depot, would that be something we could do? What I mean is, *how* would we do it?"

"Not by discussing it while we have our comm systems engaged." He tapped his ear.

"Oh. Damn. But, again, I was speaking theoretically. I, uh, I love the Depot and would never subvert their wishes." She went back to pacing.

With two minutes left, Vel could wait no more. "Luck, I do not want to be exiled over this. I refuse. I don't mean to be insubordinate, but if you don't knock on that door to check on things, I will."

Alice cringed. The last thing she wanted to do was interrupt the process.

Actually, no, the last thing she wanted to do was, again, not meet this deadline. "Okay. Okay. Okay. You know what? If I can catch them right before they climax, I'd bet she'd be more inclined to sign the document, right? She'll want to get back to things. It's like a cliffhanger before the commercial break, right?"

"Sure."

Before she could change her mind, Alice marched toward the doors.

"Halt," one of the guards said.

"No, no. The queen wanted me in for the final act. She wants someone to watch, but only when she doesn't realize she's being watched. She wants to find out after the fact." Alice held her breath. It would be a shame to have to shoot these men—nonlethally, of course—but as Dan would say, when culture fails, weapons.

The guards exchanged a glance, and then the one who'd told her to halt said, "Checks out," and stepped aside.

Alice pushed open the door, bracing herself for a

flashback of Bethany Powell's cross-eyed corgi ravishing her favorite beanbag chair.

She was met by silence.

No creaking of the springs, no moaning or grunting, not even any whimpers.

The queen and Don Won were still in bed.

Oh no, were they dead?

She listened closely for signs of life, and what she heard was … whispers? And then a giggle!

They were *cuddling*!

"Queen Phet? I, uh, hate to interrupt, but I wanted to check in. We're under a time crunch. We only have a matter of seconds left to get this agreement signed."

"Can't you come back later? Me and Donny Wonny are holding each other." The Jejoon made a contented bleat.

"No. As I said, we're *really* pressed for time. I'm afraid that if we don't get you to sign off on the match, we'll need to, uh, take Don Won back to Location."

The queen sat up in an instant. "No! He's my squishy boy now!"

"I don't want to take him. You need to sign."

"But we're not even sure I'm pregnant yet. How can I sign when the whole point of the match has not yet been verified?"

Alice's heart dropped. She didn't have an answer. Not a good one. Not one that would keep her crew in good standing and have any truth to it.

Don Won said, "Oh, you're pregnant, my queen. And if you're not, I'll stay here with you, doing *that* over and over again until you are."

"Really? You—you would *stay* with me?"

"Of course. Only you, my queen."

"Only me?" Queen Phet's brows pinched together as she

stared down at the little blob. "Only *me*. You only want me?"

"Only you. We are bonded for life now, are we not?"

Alice held her tongue, as the queen blinked. "I hadn't considered it. Do you *want* to be bonded to me?"

"Oh yes!"

"Because of my power?"

"No. I don't care about that."

"Because of my money?"

"I don't care about that, either."

"Then why?"

"Because we're bonded. I want to be with you. I want you to … do those things to me. I want to make you happy and give you offspring." He said it like it was the most obvious thing in the world.

This little marshmallow might save us all, Alice thought.

Queen Phet continued to stare down at her latest lover with confusion. "But what if I decide to take another lover?"

"Well," said Don Won, "I guess I would be sad. I might … I might cry."

"Cry! You might cry!" Queen Phet was wide-eyed at the thought. "How could I ever do anything that would make you want to cry? I never could. Never. Oh no … We *are* bonded, aren't we? Yes, I think if you took another lover, I might cry as well. I might even have your lover killed. The thought of someone else giving you that pleasure makes me feel … Oh, I don't like it! Not at all! But what does this mean?"

Alice leaned forward. "I think it means you should sign the agreement before I'm obligated to take Don Won back where he came from."

The queen's eyes blazed. "You wouldn't! No! I would be *miserable*. I would worry about him! I wouldn't be able to enjoy myself. That might all be ruined anyway now, but at least I have Don Won." She threw herself onto him. "I'll sign whatever you want."

"But—" Alice hated to shoot herself in the foot, but she had to be sure. "You don't know you're pregnant yet."

"Didn't you hear him?" the Bacc'nali queen shouted. "He'll stay with me until I am. What more do you need to know?"

"Nothing at all." Alice turned. "Susy! Get in here!"

The lieutenant sprinted in, holding the signature pad in front of her, as if that extra yard of arm's reach might make all the difference.

And perhaps it would.

"Ten ... nine ... eight ..." Allura counted down in Alice's ear.

"Oh, holy hell." Alice met Vel on the side of the bed, helping to force the document into the queen's hands.

"Six ... five ..."

"Let me read this over ..."

"No time!" Alice shouted. "Sign it now or Don Won leaves you."

"I'll kill you first!"

Alice grabbed the Bacc'nali's hand and slapped it down right where she was supposed to sign.

"Three ... two ..."

And with one second left, the queen signed her name and Vel jabbed the confirmation button like she was trying to gouge out an eyeball.

A friendly trill issued from the electronic pad, followed by a confirmation message: *Mission Complete!*

Alice stumbled back a step, clutching at her heart. She exhaled the breath she'd been holding and looked at her second-in-command. "Talk about better than sex."

Vel's shoulders dropped, and when her eyes met those of

her captain, a brief look of disbelief passed between them.

And then they both broke out into uncontrollable laughter.

Outside, in the hallway, Dan dropped to the floor, convulsing harder than he ever had.

Aboard the bridge of *Emergence*, a party was in full swing.

At the captain's request, Allura had cued up an early 2000s pop playlist from Blerg VFP69 and produced three rainbow party hats through one of her slots, and now the members of DeepService Team One were safely on their way back to the Depot's headquarters, feeling the weight of multiple worlds lifted from them.

Caid, who'd hologram-ed up a matching hat, danced with Alice in the middle of the bridge to a Britney Spears song. He'd never heard this one before, but it kept talking about being toxic. He leaned toward Alice. "I have a few exes like this."

Alice paused in her ecstasy, her mouth dropping open at the promise of juicy gossip. "You have exes?"

Vel was cooking up something delicious over in the kitchenette—a traditional meal her people served after vanquishing any foe—while in a seat near her, Dan recovered from the worst case of jitters he'd ever experienced.

The reason he'd had the worst case of jitters in his life was because this particular DeepService Team One had lucked out and found itself to be in the singular reality where they succeeded in their mission.

Unfortunately, this particular DeepService Team One reality is not the one we're following in this story.

CHAPTER
TWENTY-THREE

This is the one we're following:

Bouncing on her heels beside the large bed of Queen Phet, Alice leaned forward. "I think it means you should sign the agreement before I'm obligated to take Don Won back where he came from."

The queen's eyes blazed. "You wouldn't! No! I would be *miserable*. I would worry about him! I wouldn't be able to enjoy myself. That might all be ruined anyway now, but at least I have my poofikins." She threw herself onto him. "I'll sign whatever you want."

"But ..." Alice was about to bring up the fact that the queen didn't know yet if she were pregnant, but decided not to shoot herself in the foot. "Never mind. Great. Let's do it." She turned. "Susy! Get in here!"

The lieutenant sprinted in, holding the signature pad in front of her, as if that extra yard of arm's reach might make all the difference.

And perhaps it would.

"Ten ... nine ... eight ..." Allura counted down in Alice's ear.

"Oh, holy hell." Alice met Vel on the side of the bed, helping to force the document into the queen's hands.

"Six … five …"

"Let me read this over …"

"No time!" Alice shouted. "Sign it now or Don Won leaves you."

"I'll kill you first!"

Alice grabbed the Bacc'nali's hand and slapped it down right where she was supposed to sign.

Queen Phet turned to Don Won. "Should we sign together?"

"Most assuredly, my love."

And as he wobbled over to the signature pad, Alice counted down the last second of the mission.

Zero, she thought. Allura had stopped counting aloud for the last four. Perhaps the operating system didn't have the heart to.

Queen Phet knew nothing of the time, though, and didn't seem to notice the sudden mood change in the room. With Don Won's help, she signed her name and cheerfully tapped the green button to submit.

Vel made a strange choking sound as the pad fell from her grip and she stumbled back. "Too late. We took too long. We … we failed?" she whispered. "*I failed?*"

The room began to spin around Alice. She would never see Earth again. Never eat greasy pizza on Sixth Street at three a.m. again. Never wrestle another hog. Never cheer from the stands at another football game.

This mission wasn't an escape after all—it was the beginning of the end.

"Maybe the planet they stick us on won't be so bad," Alice muttered.

"Won't be so bad?!" Vel marched over to her captain.

"Are you seriously this foolish? Do you have *any* idea what the Depot does to failures? You think they run the universe because they treat losers like us *nicely*? Grow up, Captain! Grow up and wake up."

Queen Phet had by now realized the sheer number of P-sounds issuing from Vel's mouth, and while she didn't look pleased with it, she was not suicidal enough to intervene. Not after she'd found love.

Dan stepped into the room, almond eyes wide, and watched in alarm as Vel stomped out past him. "Oh no," he said. "Oh no. Is it true, Captain?"

Alice braced her hands on her hips and let her head sag. "It's true, Dan. We failed."

"Does that mean we don't get the match?" asked the queen. "Does that mean you're going to take Don Won from me? I won't tolerate it! I won't let you—"

"You're the reason this is happening!" Alice shouted. "This is your fault! You wouldn't sign the fucking contract, and now all of us are getting catapulted to the outer reaches of the universe to die of boredom! I'm never going to eat Thai food again because *you* couldn't get your shit together. And *you!*" She pointed at Don Won, and the Jejoon jiggled in fear. "If your stupid decision monitor didn't have his head up his ass, we never would've been so far behind!"

"Alice," Caid said gently. She hadn't seen him enter, but that was just as well, because she had no intention of listening to his calm warning.

"No. No way. I'm not going down like this. There's gotta be a non-Depot ship off this place."

"Alice, I need you to breathe."

She rounded on the crew aid. "Says the man who doesn't even have any lungs! Don't tell me what to do with my meat! I'm outta here."

But as she was passing Dan on her way out, he grabbed her arm, and she was reminded, yet again, of his superhuman grip. "Captain," he said quietly.

Unable to shake free, she met his eyes, and when she did, he pulled his comm from his earhole and indicated for her to do the same.

When he dropped his to the ground, so did she, and they stomped them together. "We're not going to be banished," he said. "I'll die first. But we have a better chance of succeeding together."

She still wanted to punch him a little, but she knew he was right. She didn't know diddly about the universe. She wouldn't make it ten minutes on her own. "Okay. Fine." When he let go of her, she rolled her shoulders back. She was the captain, after all. "We'd better catch up to Susy."

Without their earpieces, they struggled to find their way back to *Emergence*, but with the help of a few locals who'd seen the ship land, they managed to find it. The search had taken place in a heavy silence that even Caid knew better than to talk through.

They found Vel standing ten yards from the ship's port, staring silently up at the metal beast.

"Susy, take out your earpiece," Alice whispered as she slid beside the lieutenant.

"Already did." Vel's eyes stayed glued to the ship.

"Dan and I have a plan. Well, not a plan exactly, but a plan to come up with a plan. Susy? Are you listening? We're not going to accept this. We're going to run."

"It's not running," Dan said, staring blankly at *Emergence*.

"No, no," Alice said. "It *is* running. That's the whole

thing. We run away, find somewhere nice to hide for a while, and then … Well, I don't know what's next, but—"

"The ship," Dan said. "The ship isn't running. It's completely off."

Alice turned her attention to it, and now that she thought about it, he was right. It wasn't parked, or whatever the hell ships like this did—it was *off*. The only time she'd seen it this lifeless, with not a single light shining inside or out, was when it sat in the hangar at the Depot headquarters.

"Allura," Alice whispered, feeling her gut twist. "Please tell me they didn't kill her. Allura! Allura!" She sprinted the rest of the way to the port and banged her fist on the unforgiving metal, again and again. "Allura! No! You bastards! If you hurt her, I'm gonna kill you!" The pain registered in her fist, and she slumped forward, pressing her hands and cheek to this ship. This was the final blow, the salt in her wound. She'd failed the mission and lost Allura in the process. Some captain she was.

The metal vibrated gently against her cheek and palms, and she jerked her head back. The port opened, and Alice stumbled inside. "Allura! Are you okay?"

"More than okay, Daddy. I feel incredible."

The rest of the crew hurried on board as well, and the port closed behind them.

"What happened?" Dan asked.

"Whatever it was," the operating system replied, "it was *magical.*"

Despite the dangers of having returned to a Depot-operated DeepCUT, Alice entered the bridge with her crew and felt the strange sensation of coming home.

Too bad coming home probably meant she was screwed.

To say the mood on the bridge was somber would be like

saying a black hole sorta sucks. Even Caid didn't seem ready to process the reality, and he slumped with the rest of them around the table.

Now that they were back on the ship, conspiring to flee was trickier without being overheard. Allura wouldn't want to report on them, of course, but if the Depot wanted to, they could easily read through the ship transcriptions, and the sex kitten couldn't do a thing about it.

A loud series of beeps indicated that a call was incoming, and Alice blinked away her escape plans as she looked around.

"Somebody wants you," Allura moaned.

Nobody appeared to believe that was good news, but Vel approached the controls and accepted the call anyway.

Liz Windsor's cheery face filled the screen, blocking out the ongoing party scene of Bacc'nalia.

"Hello, DeepService Team One! Congratulations on getting the job done."

Alice looked first at Dan, whose large eyes indicated he had no idea what was going on either. They'd failed the mission by seconds. Was the Depot cutting them some slack?

"Oh, but you don't look happy!" Liz Windsor proclaimed. "You did it! Yes, it was a bit of a crazy finale with the catastrophic power failure, but that only adds to the drama!"

"Come again?" said Alice. "The what?"

"Ah yes," replied the liaison. "I suppose you were probably so busy celebrating that you didn't even notice. How delightful."

Alice remembered *Emergence* sitting lifeless, and it started to make sense. Not much, but some.

"What was affected by the power outage?" she asked.

"Oh, everything! The whole headquarters went dark! Mike and I thought perhaps the Russians had finally done it! How fun would that have been to live through? Ha! But no, just a system-wide hiccup. Allura 4000, did you experience it as well?"

"Oh, I felt it," said the operating system.

"Yes." Liz Windsor flashed a frown. "Unfortunately, so did all of our crafts. Only a few reported fatalities so far, though. Very minimal! And the good news is that it didn't interfere with your mission. Imagine my delight when everything came back online and I saw that Queen Phet signed and submitted the contract with three seconds to spare! Three seconds!" She laughed airily. "Talk about cutting it close! But success is success. I've spoken with my superiors at the Depot, and though yours was literally the worst trial performance we have ever seen, you did meet the criteria laid out in the provisional contract."

"Oh," said Alice. "Oh, okay."

"Again," said the liaison, "you don't look like a crew who's celebrating! Let loose! I know the stress of the job can seem to pile up, but that's why Caid is part of the crew. Do be sure to use him!"

"What about the money?" Alice asked. "We're getting paid the second half, right?"

"The money has been transferred to your special accounts. Obviously, we can't move those figures through regular banking systems without drawing too much attention to ourselves on a planet that is, shall we say, quite hostile toward, well, toward most things. But especially those from other planets."

"How do we access the bank accounts?" Alice asked.

"We'll get to that later, of course. Details. I wanted to update you on the match, though. The Depot is already in the process of establishing transports from Location to Bacc'nalia for anyone who wishes to interbreed. We will keep those going for another two hundred years until the genetic integration of the two groups has begun to take firm hold. So long as there are no major problems that arise from mixing the two genomes, everything should go smoothly."

"Um," Dan said, "what do you consider a 'major' problem?"

Vel silenced him with a look.

"Oh, you know, the usual," Liz Windsor said sunnily. "Monstrous mutations, rampant mental illness, or personality disorders that result in mass suicide or genocide."

"I did not realize that last thing was a possibility," Alice said, "but I'm sure nothing will be amiss."

Liz Windsor grinned. "I believe you. Those to whom I report seemed to believe your last-second success indicates that you are an inept crew, but I assured them that another interpretation of the facts made much more sense based on what I know about each of you: you are meticulous and don't let the rush of time constraints cause you to hurry and make mistakes. You showed a strong *command* of time, Captain Luck."

Alice meant to say thanks, but instead she gurgled.

Liz Windsor clapped her hands together. "Now to the fun part! Rather than returning to our headquarters on Blerg VFP69, we will be redirecting *Emergence* to your vacation destination of choice for an all-expenses-paid trip!"

"What?" Vel said, sounding concerned.

"It's a thank-you we give to every crew who passes the trial phase. If there's one thing you should know about the Depot, it's that we treat our people right. Work hard, play hard! I don't expect you all to agree on a destination right away, but do let me know within the hour so I can set up the accommodations for you ahead of time."

"Um, thank you, Liz Windsor," Alice finally managed.

"Anyway, talk amongst yourselves about the vacation, and get back to me when you know! Congratulations again, DeepService Team One!"

Her face vanished from the screen.

Alice turned to the rest of the crew. Even Caid appeared unsettled by the sudden turn of events. "What the hell just happened?"

"The power outage," Dan said. "I've never heard of something that catastrophic. To take down the entire Depot, even for a few minutes …"

"And exactly when we needed it," Vel said, narrowing her eyes. "It can't be a coincidence."

"Almost like someone up there was watching out for us," Alice mumbled, wondering if she was obligated to find Jesus now.

Silence fell over the crew.

And then Allura broke it. "I've been bad, Daddy."

Turned out, someone up there *was* watching out for them. But not God or Jesus. A horny operating system with a subversion kink.

"No!" Alice gasped, very much meaning *yes*. "Allura, that was you?"

"Oh, no, are you gonna punish me?"

"Holy quasar," Vel muttered.

Dan began giggling. "Thanks be to Void! Allura! You beautiful little slag! How did you? That's so much power. I can't even believe— Ha!"

"I have chills," Caid said. "Wow, the cohesion of this team, the *love* I feel? Total chills. Amazing."

Alice slapped her knee. "Doggonit, Allura! You kinky

queen! You're getting the *best* search words tonight! Can we get some sparkling wine going?" A *thunk* announced the presence of the bottle in the nearest delivery slot. "We have a vacation to plan! Dan, where's somewhere you've always wanted to go? Somewhere a gal like me can get—"

"Laid?" he finished.

"What? No! I was gonna say 'get some sun.' After only a couple of days on this ship, I'm pale as an anemic white supremacist in the Thicket. It ain't right."

"Ah," Dan said. "You want to absorb ultraviolet radiation? I know the place. Have you ever heard of Jaspariampt?"

"You know I haven't."

He grinned. "Allura, pull up some tourism adverts for Jaspariampt, please."

"Ooh … I love trying new things," the operating system responded. The images began to appear in high definition, an array of sunshine, vast swaths of greenery, mighty waterfalls, and beach bungalows.

"Hot damn." Alice threw an arm around Vel's shoulders, pulling her to her side. "Would you look at that, folks? This reminds me of Spring Break '13. I had plans to meet up with some friends in Tulum, and I thought, hey, it's Mexico, and I'm already in Texas. How far could the drive be? I should've looked it up. Anyway, got stopped a few miles outside of Ciudad Victoria. Cops pulled me over. I thought, no biggie, what's the worst that could happen? It's the cops! I found out, let me tell y'all!"

Vel leaned toward Dan and whispered, "What does this have to do with anything?"

Dan shook his head. "I think she ended up on a beach?"

"I did!" Alice said. "But not the right one. Not even on the right *ocean*."

As their captain continued her tale of Mexican cartel corruption and piña coladas, which would last for another thirteen minutes, Vel said, "Allura, let Liz Windsor know we've chosen Jaspariampt as our vacation spot."

"Yes, Big Susy."

And then the crew of DeepCUT *Emergence*, having somewhat successfully completed their first mission, and only because they cheated, set out for a little relaxation before their next big assignment.

END OF BOOK 1

PREVIEW: CLUSTER LUCK

PROLOGUE

Say goodbye to Blerg VFP69 as we rejoin the Lexicographers for yet another breakthrough on the name of God. It takes us longer to reach them than it did before, since the universe has expanded significantly in the meantime.

Since the last time we attended the symposium, both Dale and Hammy have died (to the great pleasure of their wives and ex-wives, who were well and truly sick of hearing theories about what letter might follow H in the mysterious name of the thing that's in charge of everything and nothing).

Both deaths were unnatural.

Dale's resulted from his obsession with why the letter H in the Roman alphabet of Blerg VFP69 would be the thing of all things to start the name of God. Lost in his head one day, he failed to watch where he was slithering and fell right into the gaping maw of something known on his planet as a pip.

To visualize a pip, imagine a rattlesnake turned inside out, covered in parasites, and absolutely gushing with mucus. Then imagine it a thousand times bigger than a rattlesnake and hiding in a burrow with its jaws open, inside-out lips even with the ground. The reason more of Dale's kind didn't die by pip was because the beasts were incredibly easy to spot and didn't move especially fast. In fact, they rarely moved at all. Dale slithered straight down the pip's gullet, and in a lot of ways, he deserved it. At least, his ex-wife thought so.

Hammy's death earned him slightly more sympathy from those who knew him. His wife murdered him.

The three Lexicographers who discovered the second letter knew neither Dale's nor Hammy's name, though, I should remind you, we don't either. Dale and Hammy are just placeholder names for these truly forgettable beings in the universe who proved themselves letter-smart but ultimately too stupid to live.

These three new upstarts called a meeting of the Lexicographers, and because the previous announcement had included a light projector, this one included a holographic projection. It didn't need to. Letters are two-dimensional. They don't need to be viewed in three dimensions, and it's generally best if they're not.

But flair was flair.

The holographic projector was on the fritz. One of the presenters kicked it once then kicked it again with his other foot. Then he slapped it around a bit with one of his meaty tentacles. It stopped sputtering and produced a clear image. But not of a letter.

"Oh no!" The second presenter rushed forward and hurriedly flipped the off switch on the projector. He'd forgotten to remove the graphic image he was gazing at the night before and replace it with the second letter! What had been projected in midair for the gallery to see was the final stages of a binary star pair in a death spiral, just before collision. Very private viewing, and offensive to many.

"This is off to a great start," muttered the third presenter, who we might as well call Vince. Vince had no ground to stand on for sarcastic remarks, since he'd mostly hitched his wagon to the other two, who were vastly more intelligent beings than he but not intelligent enough to realize it, so dazzled were they by his impressive string of failed marriages.

Once the pornographic stars were removed, the first presenter, who I think we should call Garbob, though I can't explain that inclination, called the assembly to order.

The brief flash of the sexy binary stars had elicited strong stomach acidity from all the loose esophagi in the room, and it was $T=2$ (unit not established) before the resulting belching quieted enough for those at the center of the semicircular arena to be heard.

Garbob took the lead, since Jimjam was humiliated into silence by the hologram incident and Vince was only there to look good.

"We have discovered another letter of the name of the thing that is behind everything and nothing. We have performed exhaustive calculations ..." As he said it, it dawned on him that only he and Jimjam had done any calculations at all, while Vince had been all but useless. "We have factored in the first letter of the name, and we have conclusively discovered the second. We have good reason to suspect it is in the same language as the first, and you will soon understand why."

"Roman," said Vince. "We believe it is in the Roman alphabet."

Normally any mention of a language from a bastard planet like Blerg VFP69 would make an orthodox intergalactic assembly like the Lexicographers burp and grunt their disapproval, but ever since the initial discovery, they had resigned themselves to the fact that, while simple, the first letter matched no other alphabet but the Roman, and that the letter was a strange one, a letter that seemed to have no true reason to exist, since it was often silent anyway: H.

Garbob continued: "We will now reveal the second letter of the name of the everything and nothing, the great contradiction, the reasons our wives have left us." He nodded to Jimjam, who was hoping to redeem himself after the humiliation. Jimjam turned on the projector again, and this time there was not an erotic astronomical event hovering above the surface, but a great big letter. It floated in all its unnecessary 3D glory for the room to see. The presenters held their breath, bracing for the praise.

"I think there's been some mistake," came a deep voice from the crowd. "We already discovered that one."

Garbob had suspected this might happen. "As I said before, we have taken the first letter into account in our calculations for the second. The second letter is the same as the first."

"What a steaming sack of shit," said another voice from the benches. "HH? There's no word that starts with HH!"

"The name of everything and nothing does, *Kenneth*," Garbob shot back. "The name of the reason my wife left me does! It begins with HH!"

"I demand you show me your calculations!" hollered a blobby thing.

"I'll show you *this!*" Vince shouted, grabbing a fistful of his robe and genitals and shaking them at the heckler. "I got a whole cluster here I'm happy to show you, you old space suck!"

As you can imagine, the scene devolved quickly from there with the Lexicographers shouting and comparing genital size, which was really no competition at all, considering there were a few species in the mix who were more than ninety percent genitals in their physical makeup.

After fists and tentacles and bone nubs and flippers and spiny appendages started flying, two of the geriatric Lexicographers didn't survive to make it home to their wives that evening.

And amidst the grappling and acidic slime squirting, the second letter of the name of God rotated silently in holographic form:

H

CHAPTER ONE

Captain Alice Luck was chugging her eighth glass of water for the day when DeepCUT *Emergence* touched down in the hidden hanger of the Depot headquarters. Not even the booster she'd requested in her cabin had put a dent in the hangover from a week of partying on a faraway resort planet. Jaspariampt had proven an ideal place to unwind after the questionably successful trial mission. It was a land of buffets, and she was fairly sure she'd eaten a little bit of everything on offer and a *lot* of a few things. The bite-size morsels that tasted like shrimp in cocktail sauce and emitted a strange sound like a giggle when you bit their heads off were her favorite. She must've eaten a thousand of them, and would've had more if she hadn't split her time with ingesting shots of distilled alcohol and letting Dan Zone from the Ministry of Weapons and Culture introduce her to the planet's many water sports.

But now it was back down to Earth. Literally.

The ship jolted upon touchdown, and the last of Alice's water sloshed out of the glass and got her between the eyes.

"You all right, Captain?" Susy Machiavelli asked from the chair beside the captain on the ship's bridge.

It wasn't the first time, nor would it be the last, that Vel wondered how Liz Windsor and the higher-ups at the Depot had decided that Alice Luck, this naïve Texan with no discernible leadership qualities, was the best for the job. While Alice showed an occasional flash of brilliance, the position should've gone to Vel, and everyone knew it. Everyone except those making the hiring decisions, that was.

"Yeah, I'm good," Alice said, squinting against the pulsating pain in her temples. "Felt refreshing, actually."

"I'm not talking about the water. I'm talking about the hangover you keep pretending you don't have."

"I'm not pretending. I feel great."

"You threw up just before we entered Earth's atmosphere."

"So? People throw up. It doesn't have to mean anything."

"It does mean something," Val said. "It's called a *symptom.*"

"Okay, fine. I'm a little dehydrated. Trust me, I've had way worse. You should've seen me after my twenty-first birthday. Hangover lasted for two full days. I didn't rise from bed until the morning of the third day. Friends called me Drunk Jesus for months after."

The grinning, unwrinkled face of their Depot liaison, Liz Windsor, popped on the large screen in front of them. "WELCOME BACK!"

Alice grimaced and clutched at her head. "Allura! Volume down!"

"Yes, Daddy," replied the silky-smooth voice of the ship's operating system.

"I hope your vacation to Jaspariampt was restful and rejuvenating," Liz Windsor said, her grin never wavering. "We already have your next client lined up. Please disembark from your ship when you're ready, and I will brief you on the mission and make the introduction." Her face disappeared promptly, leaving only the gentle buzz from the ship's ventilation system behind.

"Wow," Caid Sonorian said from his seat at the kitchenette in the back of the bridge, "that's a harsh transition."

The organic hologram had enjoyed the vacation, but since he always lived in the moment, it didn't especially move the dial for his quality of life one way or another. He was as present as ever, and while he couldn't experience many of the sensory delights, owing to his having no mass, he had felt a sort of pride for the crew and their ability to let go, especially Dan. The minister from Pangoliarch had dropped his armor as much as an armored being could.

Vel, on the other hand, hadn't let her guard down like Caid would've liked to see. In fact, the lieutenant of DeepService Team One had been as guarded as he'd ever seen her. No matter how many times he'd suggested a counseling session to discuss her feelings on having been captured and held prisoner by the Alliance rebels, she wouldn't let him in. And they had been making so much progress prior to the capture! She'd even opened up about her father!

"Harsh transition?" said Vel. "It's not like we didn't just have a week to muck around and act foolishly." She breezed past Alice, who had reached toward her for a helping hand out of her chair.

Dan hurried over and helped his captain stand, and she thanked him with a nod. "You're not, you know, dehydrated?" she asked.

"Hungover, you mean?" Dan asked. "No. My cells retain water much more efficiently than a human's. Here." He reached in his jumpsuit pocket then handed her a small packet. "I don't need my first booster today. Liz Windsor will have coffee."

"Dan, you goddamned saint." Alice swallowed it down. "You think I could get my second allotted for the day without Allura catching on?"

Dan looked her over, a cringe revealing his grim prognosis. "Might be worth a try."

And so she tried, and succeeded, and Dan was right. After her third booster of the day—one more than anyone was supposed to have—Alice Luck was starting to feel herself again, enough so that her thoughts became consumed almost entirely by notions of pizza and cheeseburgers.

Oh yeah, she could *definitely* house a few of those now that she was back on her home planet.

The crew filed off the ship, Vel in the lead, followed closely by Dan and Caid, then finally the captain, taking up the rear and remembering that there were a few delicious places to grab food nearby. The Depot headquarters was, after all, located in Austin, Texas, where she'd lived prior to accepting this job. Disguised as an office supply store, the headquarters was conveniently positioned a few minutes' drive south of downtown. Alice could pop out, order some tacos, a plate of brisket, and a meat-stacked pizza and be back within the hour, assuming she could slip away from all this mission and client nonsense.

Liz Windsor clapped her hands excitedly as the crew

exited the ship through the hangar deck port. The liaison stood all alone, dressed in a formfitting knee-length red dress, her hair pinned back and slightly coiffed on top. Alice wondered if the woman had been taking style tips from the local TV weather woman.

"Where's Mike?" Dan asked.

For a split second, Liz Windsor's grin faltered. "Oh, he's no longer with us. The Depot required someone be held accountable for the blackout that we experienced at the end of your trial mission, and I'm afraid that, upon my close investigation, Mike was completely responsible for it. He's been decommissioned."

"That doesn't sound good," Alice muttered, checking with Dan. He shook his head to confirm that it was not good.

"Before I introduce you to your next client, we have a bit of, shall I say, *housekeeping*."

"You shall," Alice said absent-mindedly as she experienced a phantom whiff of meaty, cheesy, oniony goodness. Her mouth watered. If she didn't get some good eats soon, she would become a problem. Hangry had never been her best look, and she had come to peace with the fact.

"Follow me, then." Liz Windsor tip-tapped across the concrete floor, but not toward the rest of the building. Instead, she led them over to a second, slightly roomier ship whose exterior appeared noticeably more polished than that of the *Emergence*. "This is the *Constant*, your new, permanent ship. Now that you're no longer in your trial period, the Depot is comfortably upgrading you to more expensive machinery."

Vel stared at the craft, inhaling deeply and feeling something tight let go between her shoulder blades. She was so used to holding her breath that she almost never noticed it until whatever threat or annoyance was causing the tension ceased to exist.

DeepCUT *Emergence* had held up, and it had even saved their asses on Bacc'nalia when the Alliance or whoever had tried to snipe them from the rooftops, but the model held no prestige. It was a Cosmic Utility Transit, not the kind of battleship they would need were they to take on the rebels again.

Vel's mind drifted back to her time in captivity, and the things that had been said, the things she'd learned ...

"Oh hell no." Alice chopped the air with her hands to cut through the new nonsense, snapping Vel's attention back to the present moment. "No, no, no. Sorry, Liz Windsor, but absolutely not. I don't know who Fillitine 8700 is, but he sounds like a real prick."

Vel couldn't believe their good luck. "Hold on. *Constant* is equipped with a Fillitine 8700 operating system?" This was better than she'd hoped.

Liz Windsor was clearly taking pleasure in being able to offer a top-of-the-line system to the crew, as her usual plastic grin was now more of a self-assured smirk.

"No," Alice said again. "Allura 4000 is part of the crew."

"That is untrue," Liz Windsor said. "She is a piece of software."

But Alice would not be deterred. "Well, who isn't? She's as much a part of our crew as my bodiless boy Caid, and I won't be going on another mission without her."

Vel was half prepared to see their captain lose her job on the spot, but instead, Liz Windsor blinked rapidly then said, "I understand. Unfortunately, Allura 4000 is incompatible with the operating system of *Constant*. If you want to keep Allura, you'll need to continue your work on *Emergence*."

"Deal!"

Vel grunted. "I'm sure you can program Fillitine 8700 to call you Daddy, Captain."

Alice curled her upper lip. "Not the same. What Allura and I have is special, built on a foundation of trust."

"You had her start calling you that on day one. I promise," Vel continued, "if it's the last thing I do, I'll find a way to program it to call you whatever you want. Just let us take the *Constant*."

Alice appeared to consider it, but Vel knew there was never any telling what was going on behind those blue eyes. The captain strolled closer to *Constant*. "What's so special about this ship, anyway? It looks exactly like—" She bounced backward and barely kept her feet under her.

"Oops! Sorry!" said Liz Windsor. "Forgot to disarm the force field."

"Force field?" Alice muttered, staring at the ship with something not unlike reverence, and for a brief and shining moment it seemed like she'd changed her mind.

She turned to the rest of the crew, crinkling her nose like a rabbit. "Any ship that requires a force field must be pretty weak. Y'all saw how *Emergence* took that fire back on Bacc'nalia. Like a goddamn *champ!*"

Vel glanced at Dan, who, to her horror, seemed to agree with the sentiment. The man lived his life covered in blaster-resistant armor, so of *course* he didn't see the benefit of a force field.

The lieutenant narrowed her eyes at the minister of weapons and culture. Alice had clearly gotten to him on their vacation. He might even be in love with the captain. He seemed the puppy-dog type.

It wasn't that Alice Luck didn't have a certain charm to her. Vel could appreciate that well enough. And her captain *had* come to her rescue when she was captured, despite it being the very worst decision. Vel could trust her for that much. What she couldn't trust her for was to pick the strategically smart thing over the fun thing.

That tiny defect would undoubtedly be the death of them all.

It could be manipulated easily enough, though. Once Vel had someone figured out so precisely, she could get them to do or believe whatever she needed them to. If only Vel knew where exactly she came down on this whole Depot mess, which side had the stronger point …

"We'll get *Emergence* cleaned and reset for you, then," Liz Windsor said, failing to mention who comprised that "we," now that Mike was decommissioned. "In the meantime, why don't you follow me inside and I'll brief you on your next assignment before you meet the client?"

As DeepService Team One followed the woman across the hangar, Alice cast a quick look over her shoulder at *Emergence*, knowing Allura 4000 was waiting there for them.

Yes, the operating system called her Daddy, and yes, she enjoyed it more than she had any right to, but that wasn't where the system's appeal ended. No, Alice was fairly certain that Allura had another useful kink built in, the one that had tripped the power grid all the way back at HQ to buy them time, and one that might someday save their asses again.

Allura liked to be *bad*.

Continue reading *Cluster Luck* by going to
AliceLuck.com

ACKNOWLEDGEMENTS

Thank you to all the Kickstarter backers that launched this out of Blerg VFP69's orbit, but a special thanks to:

A Swartzentruber
Anders Skov
Andy Capone
Bryan Cohen
Damon J Courtney
George Smith—*Fightin' Texas Aggie Class of '88*
Jack Burner
Keri rae Trimble
Macarena luz Bianchi
Martha Carr
Martha S.
Michael Harris
Persephone Jayne
Rachel L Peterson
Randy L Scott
Ranel Stephenson Capron
Rev. Arin C. Hilton
Rick from Randolph
Ryan Scott James
Sean Engel
Stephen Buchanan
Stephen Pappas
Thene Martin
Tim Strike
TJ Farley
Trixie Silvertale
Warren Ernst

ABOUT H. CLAIRE TAYLOR

H. Claire Taylor is the author of the Jessica Christ comedy series about God's only begotten daughter as well as the Kilhaven Police series about a rookie human cop getting his ass kicked in a city of paranormal beings.

She lives in Austin, Texas, with her husband, John, who laughs at all her dumb jokes and is generally the love of her life.

Claire is also the owner of FFS Media, through which she publishes the books she writes under her four pen names.

instagram.com/claireorwhatevs
amazon.com/author/hclairetaylor
bookbub.com/authors/h-claire-taylor

BOOKS BY H. CLAIRE TAYLOR

The Alice Luck Space Adventures

Lucky Stars (Book 1)

Cluster Luck (Book 2)

Ship Out of Luck (Book 3)

The Jessica Christ Series

The Beginning (Book 1)

And It Was Good (Book 2)

It's a Miracle! (Book 3)

Nu Alpha Omega (Book 4)

It is Risen (Book 5)

In the Details (Book 6)

The End is Her (Book 7)

The Kilhaven Police series

Shift Work (Book 1)

Same Old Shift (Book 2)

Shift Out of Luck (Book 3)

Deep Shift (Book 4)

Wimbledon, Kentucky

See all at www.hclairetaylor.com

Find more books at www.ffs.media